# emerald elephant

# emerald elephant

# Ann Gustafson Frake

# Emerald Elephant

## by Ann Gustafson Frake

© 1997, Word Aflame Press
   Hazelwood, MO 63042-2299

Cover Design by Paul Povolni
Author's Photo by Jacqueline Frake
Cover Art: "India's Beautiful People" by Anniedeen Creel. Notecards and prints
   of this and other paintings can be purchased from Anniedeen Creel Studio,
   903 Jackson Street, Casper, WY 82601, (307) 265-8223.

All Scripture quotations in this book are from the King James Version of the
Bible unless otherwise identified.

Fiction Disclaimer: All the characters in this story are fictional with the excep-
tion of a cameo appearance by Lera, a marvelous Indian missionary evangelist.
None of my single friends do or say anything I want them to, so I'm left to make
up stories.

Printed in United States of America

Printed by

---

### Library of Congress Cataloging-in-Publication Data

Frake, Ann Gustafson.
      Emerald elephant / Ann Gustafson Frake.
         ISBN 1-56722-198-X
         I. Title.
         PS3556.R258E47      1997
         813'.54—dc21                                      97-497
                                                            CIP

---

To Bob Frake,
my marvelous husband, who still makes
all the fictional heroes seem pale and
sickly in comparison.

# ONE

**A** **CLOUD** **OF** **DUST** followed the derelict bus as it careened down a road, away from the New Delhi airport. The sun baked the people who rode inside, but the men sitting on top of the bus had umbrellas, so they enjoyed shade and breeze, making it easy to chat as they maintained their precarious balance.

Kerry, sitting inside, lifted the shining, bronze-colored braid off the back of her hot neck. Seated next to her on the bus was an elderly woman wrapped in a bright green sari, an ornate gold stud in her nose. On the woman's lap, cackling, was a large chicken. Whenever Kerry wiped her forehead and neck with her big, fluttery handkerchief, the chicken started flapping and trying to escape.

Kerry shifted her eyes away and looked around the bus, wondering if any more of humanity and the animal kingdom could squeeze themselves on, in, or around this contraption. Her shirt was sticking to her, the sweat running in rivulets down the middle of her back. If she'd had a big glass of ice and lemonade right then, it would have taken a lot of control not to pour it over her own head.

Three days ago, she had been in her office in

Columbus, Ohio. There she worked as a secretary for a geological survey firm, Geraghty and Miller.

"Could it only be three days?" Kerry murmured, "I feel as though I have lived through several Dark Ages since then."

Mr. Miller had called her into his office. "Miss Carlyle, I understand that your passport and shots are still valid since last fall's little jaunt to Burma?"

Kerry, young, competent and self-assured, occasionally acted as a courier for sensitive equipment to different countries. After all, laser equipment did not stand up well to smashing, stomping and squashing, the usual procedures for fragile equipment in the luggage-handling departments of airports.

Kerry always took the equipment with her in the plane's passenger compartment and held it on her lap. Once she even bought a ticket for a separate seat to accommodate a very large box. She made all the airport connections and passed over the soil-sample microscope (or whatever) to the waiting staff at the airport. Her longest layover to date had been thirty-four minutes, which gave her enough time to do some deep knee bends or jumping jacks before an incredibly long plane trip back. Seeing anything other than the airport terminal was not included in her job duties. However, these jaunts did break up one's week. Kerry inwardly sighed as she got ready for another cramped flight.

"Miss Carlyle, I'd like you to consider a very sensitive assignment. Your supervisor has recommended you because he has a high degree of trust in your abilities. He also said that you are very good with his three little boys when they stop by, and that is a big qualification for this trip."

"Well, I do love children. I sometimes teach Sunday school to toddlers in my home church."

"Good. You are aware that we have field people outside of New Delhi, India? Mr. Gunderson, a geologist from Stockholm, his wife, who is a biochemist, and their two little girls have a home and a small lab there. I've just received word from the American embassy that the parents have been killed in an explosion. It looks as if it was deliberately set."

Kerry was shocked into silence. Mr. Miller went on.

"Both children were playing outside the home, with their *ayah*, or baby sitter. They all heard the explosion. The older girl, who's eight, tried to run into the fire that resulted after the explosion. She burned both hands before their gardener grabbed her. She's in a New Delhi hospital now. The younger one, four years old, is staying with the ayah in the home, which for the most part was not damaged. I need someone to get those children and escort them to the United States. I need someone who can be a comfort to children in shock and grief."

"I'd be very willing to help," Kerry answered sincerely.

"The company will pick up all expenses. You'll have to leave tomorrow evening. The Indian consulate will have a special visa ready for you. They will have a messenger waiting at the gate when you change planes in Washington, D.C. You will have to sign some forms, plus show photo identification. Is it too much?"

Without hesitation Kerry answered, "No, I'm glad to go. Those poor little girls! Do you know their names?"

"The older one with burns is Danielle, and the other is Kathryn. Their mother was French, and we're trying to

11

reach her family. There is only a grandfather listed as next of kin and no one on the husband's side at all."

"You're going to need some things for yourself and the children, so here is a company charge card. Get your currency in New Delhi from the automatic teller each day. The currency rate is exact for that day, and because we have a corporate account, there is no charge for the service."

He paused. "You may also need some things, perhaps some clothing that's appropriate to this season's climate, whatever it is in India."

They both looked outside the office window to the February snow drifts, icicles, and frozen river.

"It's been known to rain there," he concluded dryly as he glanced at Kerry's beautiful wool suit, in soft pink, expensive suede heels, and perfectly arranged silk scarf in pinks and blues.

Outside his office, the enormity of the situation hit Kerry, and she was both appalled and delighted. Her adrenaline kicked in, and she started thinking of all the things that needed to be done. After leaving the office early, her work delegated to others, she made arrangements with one of her friends to get her mail and use up the contents of her refrigerator.

Then she called her mother.

"Kerry, tomorrow? Can you possibly be ready? Your father will have a fit! He's in St. Louis, at a foreign missions conference."

Kerry mentally enjoyed the picture of her father, a pastor who cared deeply for his flock, going into a dither. He would never get over his image lag of her as an incompetent thirteen-year-old.

Kerry loved her Dad "like crazy," and "crazy" was the operative word. The two of them were very much alike in temperament and drove each other nuts upon occasion.

"Kerry, you will take care of yourself?" Her mother added, "I've been praying for you."

"Well then, Mom, I'm covered from all angles." Kerry's voice was filled with tolerant amusement. God surely honored her parents' childlike faith, but it often filled her with exasperation.

Kerry set off for the Land Rover shop, a place she'd often looked through but never had enough money to buy anything from before. It was designed for the serious traveler in mind.

"I need some clothing that will be comfortable, cheerful, and bright; won't wrinkle much; and can be washed out in the sink each night."

The clerk brightened and ran to bring something out.

"A parachute? Hey, I'm not that big!" Kerry looked down at her generous curves and wished for the millionth time that she was thinner. She was unaware that she looked fine, carried herself lightly, and often got admiring looks from single men. Her attractiveness was centered in her vitality and lively curiosity. Her face was not classically beautiful, but her eyes were bright with intelligence and her manner put people at ease immediately.

"It's not a parachute. It's a peasant-style dress made from parachute material in beautiful pink with bright tropical fish appliqués. Watch!" The assistant wadded up the outfit into her fist. It collapsed down to nothing. "It's the newest thing. I'll shake it out, almost no wrinkles."

"Does it dry fast?"

"Guaranteed! Also in soft rose with pastel parrots and

icy blue with pale yellow hibiscus. Very cool and comfortable for traveling in hot places."

"I'll take all three."

"Where are you going?"

"New Delhi, India."

The girl typed the destination on a keyboard, and a printer immediately spit out a long sheet with an atlas account of the seasonal climate.

"You're lucky this isn't monsoon season; however, you can expect intermittent rain. In February India has average daytime temperatures of sixty degrees but might be higher on some days. In the evenings it will be cool, all the way down in the forties."

They both laughed at the idea of a cool evening in the forties. The wind chill in Ohio that day made it feel like twelve below zero.

"May I give you our list of recommended items to pack for this kind of destination?"

Kerry's eyes ran over the list. "This sounds like I might get wet," she said frowning. "I hate to get wet. I have an ear that hates to get wet. Oh, phooey, why'd I ever accept this assignment?"

One of Kerry's ears had given her a lifetime of problems. Many surgeries and infections later, she was ready to pour cement in that side and forget it. Moisture was to be avoided at all costs. Cotton in her pockets, huge rain hats, and big umbrellas were all part of the reality of keeping her ear dry and avoiding infections. She resisted asking the clerk if they sold tiny shower caps for ears. She always carried packs and packs of gum for the plane trips, to equalize any ear pressure changes.

She bought a pair of rubber sandals, guaranteed to

survive wading through puddles, and a huge, lightweight nylon carry-on. It had lots of pockets and a good, wide shoulder strap for carrying it. But the feature Kerry really liked was its neon pink color. There would be no danger of losing that glow-in-the dark luggage!

As Kerry surveyed the growing amount of purchases, she thought about those two little girls, all alone, missing their mom and dad.

"You wouldn't happen to have kids' clothing in that parachute material? They need to have pockets."

Loaded with outfits for everyone, all of which fit into a shoe box, Kerry left, feeling much better, and rode the escalator down to the children's department. Kerry knew she'd have limited luggage and that she could only take essentials. But essentials to little girls might be different from what an adult normally carried.

Kerry bought bright socks, underwear, and long tee-shirts in matching bright teddy-bear prints. Finally she added two children's purses, filled with wonderful items to entertain on a long trip.

Back at her apartment, Kerry stayed up most of the night packing things that seemed important into her carry-on. She put her papers, Bible, and medications into large zip-lock baggies.

Kerry took her Bible with her on all trips, from life-long habit, but rarely read it these days. She was always very busy.

The carry-on would stay with her the whole trip because she couldn't risk losing her luggage or the delay in getting it back. If everything went smoothly, she would be home within ten days. That should be enough time to pack up and ship the Gundersons' personal items from the house and anything left of business papers or equipment.

How long ago that seemed now! Kerry leaned her head against her purse, wedged into the corner against the bus window frame, and tried to catch some breeze. It felt as if someone was sandblasting her face, the wind was so hot. And this was cooler than normal? Ha! Kerry fiddled with the cotton in her ear.

She was tired. It had been over twenty-four hours since she left home, with no bed to stretch out on. Her body thought it was the morning of the next day, when in fact it was late afternoon in India.

Arriving early at the airport had meant getting up at 4:00 AM. Then there were two flight changes, one in Washington, D.C., and the other in London. Add seventeen hours of time in the air, and the sum total was an exhausted woman with very little patience left.

Abruptly, the bus stopped. A jeep had pulled in front of them, effectively stopping the vehicle's journey. The bus driver was yelling, but he stopped as an Indian police officer in a khaki uniform boarded, scanning the faces of the passengers. His eyes stopped when he spotted the only American face on board. He indicated that Kerry should follow him. He wore a pistol in a holster.

The bus, so noisy only seconds before, was now a low murmur of voices, with every eye on Kerry as she laboriously got her bag and purse and crawled over her seat partner, the chicken, and several others in the aisle.

"Marvelous," Kerry muttered, following him around the bus and toward the jeep. A big blond man, mid-thirties, was sitting in the front, foot propped up on the dash. He stood as he saw her approach, and Kerry saw that he was very handsome in a rough way. He smiled tightly and said, "Miss Carlyle, your father sent me."

Kerry's eyes grew wide with horror. She seriously considered howling and barking like a dog in frustration. Obviously, several thousand miles was not far enough to escape her father's overprotective, sometimes patronizing assistance.

Kerry gritted her teeth and said in a flat tone, "What a surprise."

"I realize you were not expecting to be greeted. I'm in New Delhi on a tourist's visa. Brother Carlyle and my father were at a missions conference together when the news came that you were on your way to New Delhi. He apparently called your employer and mentioned that you needed a good contact. Mr. Miller then decided to contract my services to aid you while you're here. Personally, I could use the financial assistance from this contract."

"Thank you for indulging my dad, but I'm fine. I'm not here to see the sights. I have a job to do, so again, thank you. I don't have any time for excursions." With a dismissive smile, Kerry turned around to get back on the bus. An officer blocked her path, and she turned back slowly, all friendliness gone from her face, one eyebrow raised in inquiry.

"I'm afraid it's not that easy, Miss Carlyle. Let me explain. I am now your business associate and transportation. Your father and Mr. Miller have arranged for me to be your watchdog this week."

This last sentence came out in a hard voice. He wasn't any crazier about the situation than she was.

Kerry's anger felt like a volcano inside, getting ready to blow. "And just exactly who are you, Mr. Dog?" Kerry asked in a bland tone.

"That's 'watchdog,' and I am usually known as Dr. Rand Dennison, but of course, since you're not on a pleasure trip, you may call me Dr. Dennison."

Kerry flushed. It was perfectly obvious to her that the handsome Dr. Dennison was in this for the green stuff. It didn't take a genius to judge the character of "Mr. Good Looking." Most women would be delighted to have him as an escort and companion. But not me! she thought. I prefer ugly, cross-eyed men with warts who are just chock full of . . . of . . . goodness, I guess.

All this time Rand had been standing in the jeep. Now he sat down and motioned for her to climb in the back. No help seemed to be forthcoming.

Kerry trudged over and threw her stuff in the back, then realized that there was no door to open. One apparently leaped over the side. Pole vaulting was a definite option here. Kerry looked around for something to stand on, put her foot on . . . anything.

Dr. Dennison spoke from the front, without so much as turning his head. "Miss Carlyle, it is becoming more and more apparent why your father and employer agreed you needed a keeper in India. Shall I call the driver to lift you into the back seat?"

Kerry considered murder and then rejected it as too good for him and thought about torture instead. Such happy thoughts! It gave her impetus to climb over into the back seat, grateful that the parachute dress was abundantly full. She was so angry that she didn't care if she looked ridiculous or not. Only two little girls stood between Dr. Dennison and his final end as far as Kerry was concerned.

Instead of reaching out and strangling him, Kerry

transferred her thoughts to her father. Reverend Carlyle had grown up in New York City and had received the Holy Ghost in his teens, after running with a few gangs. Although he was now a pastor in the heartland, he was missions minded and had traveled in many Third World countries. He was very safety oriented when it came to his single daughter, and Kerry knew it was his concern that had prompted the hire of this goon for a week.

It drove her crazy! Imagine, sticking her with God's gift to women for a week or more, plus calling her boss and talking about her like a child!

Rand, sitting in the front of the jeep, had something other than the tall, golden girl in the back seat to occupy his mind. He was going to ignore that obviously intelligent, spoiled, and articulate responsibility. Never mind that her eyes flashed green when she stood up to him. Never mind that she was so lovely and coordinated that he felt as if he were in junior high again. He was acting badly, he knew. He just wasn't expecting a model to show up. It put him off his stride. He was expecting an old, spinster-type career person. Well, he'd try to make it up to her later.

He patted his shirt pocket absently and felt the letters stuffed there. He'd picked up his mail on the way to the airport, but this driver hadn't known the back way, so he didn't have time to read it. He pulled the envelopes out now and looked at them, absently yanking his tie to the side, achieving a disheveled style that was not in the least bit becoming to him.

Rand pushed his fingers through his blond, curly hair, leaving it sticking up all over. The bills and notices were expected. His mail included one plain, typewritten envelope that had no return address.

Rand recognized it. He had two more in his hip pocket that looked just the same.

He tore open the envelope and read the contents. It was shorter than the others had been but said virtually the same thing. He pulled out two matching letters and looked at the total of three on his lap.

All three envelopes were typed on the same machine, and the messages worried Rand.

# TWO

"**NO MORE SCHOOL** or clinic! Danger! Sorrow! Death!"

Each of the letters held threats, and each had messages pasted together from advertisements that had been clipped from a British newspaper. That in itself was a clue. Whoever was sending these notes understood and spoke English. But who and why? Rand hated this sort of business.

Very tall and strong, Rand had spent much of his life in India, first as a child with his missionary parents, then on a medical tour, and finally now, by himself, establishing a clinic.

When he introduced himself to Miss Carlyle, he had not explained that while he was here on a visitor's visa in India, he was illegally doing medical work with a group of missionaries. He wanted to establish a Bible school and clinic before he no longer had access to the country.

Although he was fair by nature, all the work on the Bible school buildings left Rand more tanned than usual. He did allow himself a cursory glance every morning in the mirror, more out of habit than any real interest in his appearance.

Lately, he had noticed less hair to comb. He cut it himself, and it looked as if he did. Blissfully unaware that his glasses were ten years out of style and his clothing at least ten more, Rand often used the donated clothing that people sent, saying, "This material is like new, hardly any wear at all."

He had no idea that taken in hand, he would clean up quite nicely and look rather handsome. Handsome was not a priority. Books, equipment, medical instruments, medicine, and transportation were Rand's priorities.

"And just where are those new crates of charts for infant nutrition that came in yesterday's post?" he mumbled to himself. The threatening letters and Kerry were completely forgotten as Rand's mind moved on to the things he really cared about.

Kerry glanced at her watch and realized it had been more than twelve hours since her last meal. It felt as if it had been three days since she'd seen a rest room.

She dug into a pocket and pulled out a bag of dried mangos and pineapple that she had picked up at the airport. She had a pound of the dried fruit, and she fervently thanked God, in silence, for its availability. She'd starve before she'd request anything from that rotten man. Of course, she hadn't really counted on the insistent call of nature.

"Dr. Dennison, will we be stopping soon?" Kerry asked in a neutral voice. She waited and then realized that he had not heard her. "Dr. Dennison! May I have your valued attention, please?"

He jumped in his seat, turning around to look at her as if she had just appeared from Mars. "Excuse me, I didn't hear you," he said almost apologetically, perhaps forgetting that he was speaking to an adversary.

The thought made Kerry smile. It was the first time that she'd smiled since she met Rand Dennison and he was a bit dazzled. And then they both remembered themselves.

"Are we going to stop soon?"

"Stop? Here? Whatever for?" Rand looked puzzled.

"Stop for . . . food or supplies or gas or anything?" Kerry tried not to sound desperate.

"Oh, do you need to go to the bathroom?"

Well, Kerry would rather die before she was going to admit to such human frailty now. Normally not so sensitive, she felt her pride was on the line, and she hated to discuss any bodily functions with Dr. Dennison. Unfortunately, the urgency of the matter demanded some attention.

With great dignity she said, "I most emphatically do not. I would like a rest stop soon, thank you very much."

Rand choked back a grin and realized something. It had been a very long time since he had made any polite conversation with a pretty lady, and he was going to have to polish it up.

"Miss Carlyle, I have been remiss. We will be stopping in a moment for a rest stop before we go to the hospital. We will find your oldest charge, check her out, and then pick up her little sister. Then we'll take a bus to the outlying suburbs of New Delhi, where I am staying at a school. Mr. Miller has asked me to find accommodations for your comfort while here. I have an English lady friend who's also a doctor. She and her father have offered you a room in their home, which is next to the school. That will give you a base to get the paperwork in order so that you and your charges can leave next week. Any more questions?"

"How on earth did you know about all that?" Kerry did not pause for a breath or an answer. "And why do I stay by your school and not in the Gundersons' house? I understand that only the lab was destroyed."

"Have you forgotten that you are in India now? You may be American, but here single women are prey to every criminal in the city. Without men in the house, and half a dozen servants, I'd have to hire someone to guard you at night. Mr. Miller and I arranged the rest after he filled me in on the details. He thought I'd better know about your children and the situation before I accepted the job."

"It looks as though you have everything under control, Dr. Dennison. I can't imagine why anyone bothered to send me at all," Kerry answered sarcastically.

"Miss Carlyle, don't whine. I know very little about young children, and this is the most inauspicious time in the world to travel in India. This is India's *maha kumbh mela*. And here we are at the rest stop!"

Kerry restrained herself from saying that if they were any longer getting to the rest stop they would have experienced a most inauspicious occasion in the jeep. She exited from the jeep, using the standard form for dismounting horses, and decided that it worked fairly well with a jeep.

She raced into a little building where truck drivers paid for gasoline, got inside, and couldn't get anyone to understand what she was looking for. She raced back out and grabbed Rand's arm where he stood talking to the driver who was filling the tank with petrol.

"I can't get them to understand! Please come and tell them what I am looking for!"

Rand quickly spoke a few words to a young man at the pump, who pointed over his shoulder and didn't make eye contact with Kerry. Actually, after Rand realized what the man said, he didn't really want to make any eye contact either. He took her arm and walked toward the back of the building.

"I don't suppose you could wait until we get to the hospital in half an hour?"

"What!"

"No, I didn't think so. Well, there's a little problem."

"If I don't find a rest room soon, there's going to be a much bigger problem!"

"You must understand, in India, most regular women don't stop at truck stops. The only facilities are in a house in back."

"What does that mean, most regular women?"

"The house in back is run by . . . rough women."

"Rough women? Dr. Dennison, you are from the Stone Age. If I'm not back in a few minutes, just write to my folks. And watch that bag in the jeep. Everything I need in the world is inside."

Kerry quickly walked away from Rand, and he stood watching as she made a short walk to a ramshackle house in back and disappeared in its doorway.

He felt very apprehensive. What if they murdered her? She didn't speak anything but English; what were her chances of being understood?

In minutes, Kerry was exiting, laughing and waving back at the house. As she got nearer, Rand realized that she looked different. Her hair was down, out of its braid.

"Well, that was interesting. Those ladies wanted to see my auburn hair and just started pulling it down, out of its braid. But they were very gentle. I hurried in case their curiosity was inexhaustible. I also left my bobby pins with them, which they apparently have never seen before, as a thank-you. It seemed to please them."

Rand just kept looking at her, with that long, beautiful hair floating around her shoulders and down her back. The humidity caused the little wisps to curl around her face.

"I'm amazed at your willingness to march right into that place, Miss Carlyle."

"Well, Dr. Dennison, I'm amazed that you're amazed. Didn't you know that we're all God's children?"

Dr. Dennison did a little bow, made a flourish with his hand and proclaimed a cold, "Touché, and en garde." He was furious. "Thank you, Miss Goodwill Tour, for instructing me on prejudice!" he mumbled to himself. I wonder how she'd do with my patients who are lepers, was his uncharitable thought. He turned his back and climbed into the front seat, leaving Kerry to scramble into the back.

Back in the jeep, Kerry asked, "What is a *maha kumbh mela?*"

"Every twelve years or so, Hindu astrologers calculate a perfect time for millions of Hindus, of all castes, classes and practices, to wash away their sins and pray to escape the endless circle of reincarnation."

"So?"

"The problem is that the holiest spot to achieve this is where the Ganges and Tamuna Rivers meet. You'd better not get in anyone's way on their pilgrimage. Almost all of the Hindus in north-central India will be using some part of the Grand Trunk Road, which stretches from Calcutta to northern Peshawar, to get to the confluence of the rivers. New Delhi is right on the Grand Trunk Road, and we are in New Delhi."

As if to prove Rand correct, an enormous group of men with ash smeared across their foreheads pushed past the jeep as it stopped. The men carried a large ornate litter, garlanded with long chains of yellow flower blossoms. Marigolds, perhaps, Kerry thought as she watched. In the litter sat an old man, nearly hidden in his robes.

"That is a *mahant*, or a guru. His disciples are taking him to the rivers."

Kerry hated to admit it, but the large group, chanting as they rushed forward, frightened her. The city of Delhi reminded her of parts of New York City. There was not the same level of technology, but they did share enormous masses of people, all intent on their own destinations and plans.

She gazed around her, inhaling the miserable exhaust of the other vehicles on the road. Buses, trucks, and a few cars vied for road space with animals, bicycles, handcarts, and of course, pedestrians.

Kerry saw thin, coughing men pulling rickshaws, sometimes with a bicycle. Rand said that many of them had tuberculosis. Just as many people traveled on foot, running in and out among the vehicles and livestock. There did not seem to be any order or traffic system, and Kerry gasped as children darted in front of their jeep dozens of times.

Suddenly, she felt a hand on the back of her neck. Someone in back of her pushed her head down!

Kerry jerked around in the jeep. There stood an elephant of huge proportions, his ear tips looking lighter and freckled from age. A man sat perched behind the great beast's head.

The animal's trunk came up, and the tip, soft and careful as a finger, touched the top of her head. She laughed and reached out to give her spontaneous friend a piece of dried mango. He delicately took it and put it in his mouth.

A bus pulled along beside, and the passengers, on top and inside, called to the elephant, trying to touch it with outreached hands. Women, with dots in the middle of their foreheads and parts of their hair painted red with henna, held up their babies to see, smiling.

"The passengers are saying that you are very lucky, Miss Carlyle. There are not many elephants used for work in the cities anymore. Twenty-five years ago, when I was a child, elephants were more common than cars on the Grand Trunk Road."

"You grew up in India, then?" questioned Kerry.

"Yes, my parents were missionaries."

"But you are just visiting now. Right?" He did say tourist's visa, didn't he? Kerry tried to remember.

Changing the subject, Rand pointed at the elephant. "The palace owns most of the trained elephants in New Delhi and uses them during Hindu holy days. Elephants have the largest brains, proportionately, of any animal. Many a trainer, or elephant *mahout*, claims they have superior intelligence. This one is considered a sacred elephant, used for parades, and he seems to like you. Of course, I might like you too, if you gave me a piece of that dried fruit," Rand concluded.

Kerry was feeling so much better after finding a nice friend, even if it was an elephant, that she decided to be magnanimous. "I'd be happy to share with you and the driver. Please call me Kerry."

"Thank you. Please call me Rand, and the driver will not eat anything from you or me. We would ruin his caste. He is a Brahmin and has strict dietary rules. He is the younger brother of a chef at one of the hotels. He is only driving us today as a favor."

Whether or not the driver understood was a mystery to Kerry, for he never looked in her direction.

Just then the jeep passed by a large group of horribly crippled children. As the traffic slowed, they ran out to the road. One particularly scarred, twisted girl was pushed right up to Kerry, the little hand pathetically reaching out and obviously asking for money. Kerry scrambled in her pocket for change, but the jeep began to pull away and the children were left behind.

Frantically, Kerry shouted above the traffic noise, "Go back; they need some money."

Rand just shook his head negatively.

Kerry could not believe it. He was a monster! Here were the poor, the hungry, and the naked, and this "doctor" wasn't interested in helping. Well, it just confirmed her initial impression that he was only in this for the money.

Kerry punched him on the shoulder to get his attention, and none too gently. "I said they need money and food. What's the matter with you?"

Oh, she had his attention now.

"Aren't we being rather quick to judge, Miss Carlyle? We never give money to children in begging rings because they do not get food or benefit from it. The ringleader will just buy more children to mutilate, so that he can have a bigger begging ring."

Kerry's face lost all its color, and her eyes grew wide with horror. She felt her breath whoosh out of her lungs as though she'd been punched.

Rand watched her reaction guiltily. He should have anticipated her concern. It must seem heartless to her to leave those children behind. How could he ever explain all the legal ramifications, let alone practical ones, that kept him from taking half a million begging people, in this city alone, home with him? They needed everything in the world, and truly only God could ever, ever supply all those needs. He knew that a Savior was the only solution he could offer on a grand scale.

"Please don't cry. In the neighborhood of the school we try to intervene and offer help to children. Dr. Greyson, with whom you'll be staying, has a medical clinic for the neighborhood every morning from eight to ten."

"Is she your fiancee?"

"No! Of course not. I don't have any time for that sort of thing," Rand said crossly, as if that concluded any discussion. He turned around and looked intently at the traffic.

Kerry rolled her eyes. Obviously it was a sore spot with his high and mightiness. Well, she could understand. There were certain questions that put her own back up. Kerry just hoped he didn't think she had any designs on him. In fact, the phrase "last man on earth" was running through her thoughts rather frequently.

They pulled up in front of the Mother of Redeemer Hospital. It did not look very modern. In fact it seemed like something out of Victorian times.

Kerry and Rand walked up to the front desk of the

high-ceilinged entryway. All the nuns in the hospital wore the flowing white and black habits that were no longer popular in the United States. The sister at the desk spoke beautiful English and smiled when Rand told them who they wanted to see. She immediately called an orderly to take them to the correct ward.

The whole place reminded Kerry of Florence Nightingale's hospital. Everything was clean, with lots of open archways and windows and very old-fashioned equipment. In fact, with all the long nun's robes, one of them could have passed for Florence herself.

On the children's ward, small patients were out of bed and playing quietly. Many had casts on their legs and arms, and it was easy to see that this particular ward had injuries that were not life threatening.

The only blond head in the room sat looking out of the window, not playing or joining any other children. One of the sisters came over and nodded toward her.

"We are afraid Danielle has gone into a depression. Her hands were hurt, with second degree burns, when she rushed into the fire after the explosion. The gardener held her back, but she was very upset. She is sometimes delusional."

"Delusional?" Kerry asked, her heart aching for Danielle, who had seen her parents die.

"She thinks her parents are still alive."

"Alive? Now?"

"Yes, she keeps asking us to help her find them. She says that bad men took them. The psychiatrist on staff says it is a common coping mechanism. He recommends that we not encourage her, but ignore it until she is able to accept their deaths."

"You go over and I'll wait here," Rand said. He didn't have a clue what to say to the child. In the rural villages, when he held clinics, the parents always spoke for their children.

Kerry and the nun walked over. Rand watched as Kerry spoke to Danielle, not moving in too fast or smothering her with pity. They started putting the child's possessions into a little paper bag. There wasn't much.

She wore a shirt, long enough to be a dress, with the sleeves rolled up, and it was easy to see that it had been donated by the hospital. Her shoes still had soot marks on them. Her blond hair was matted and parts of it looked singed, even though her face was clean.

"We had to cut off her clothing, I'm afraid," said the nun. "We couldn't get it off over her hands."

The hands in question were still wound with big white bandages, and the nun was explaining what treatment and salves they would need.

"Danielle, perhaps you will let Miss Carlyle work on your hair when she has a chance."

Danielle looked at them, said, "I'll let my mom do it," and walked away from Kerry and the nun.

The sister spoke confidentially to Kerry. "She won't let us touch it. We wanted to wash it and cut out the snarls, but she became hysterical. Perhaps when she's out of the hospital she'll feel better."

Danielle, meanwhile, headed straight toward Rand. "Who are you?" she asked, looking up at his great height.

"I'm Rand; who are you?"

"Danielle. Am I going with you?"

"Yes, you and Miss Carlyle and your little sister are coming with me for a while."

"Would you carry me?"

The request startled Rand. All the eight-year-old boys that he knew would rather die than ask anyone to carry them. And all the eight-year-old girls he'd seen were too shy to talk with him.

"Are you too ill to walk?" he asked, taking in her slight frame and thin face.

"No, I just wanted you to carry me for a while," Danielle answered defensively.

It finally occurred to Rand that Danielle might be very frightened. Her parents were gone, her destination was unknown, and her future was uncertain.

Give the kid a break, he thought. "Good, I was hoping you'd ask. I want to show that pretty lady just how strong I am." He winked before he gathered her up. She put her head on his shoulder, bandaged arms sticking straight out behind his head, legs dangling almost to his knees.

By now, they both had Kerry's attention. She raised her eyebrows in inquiry. Rand just grinned and shrugged, immensely pleased with himself for some reason he couldn't identify.

# THREE

**KERRY FELT LIKE** a native in a bad Tarzan story, carrying her tote, her purse, and a brown paper bag out to the bus as Danielle pointedly ignored her and clung to Rand's neck with a wrestler's grip.

Danielle was reacting to shock. Rand reminded her of the strong, calm man that she was accustomed to relying on in life, her dad. It seemed correct to her that Rand was going to be the answer to her problems. The woman, Miss Carlyle, was kind, but Danielle wanted strength right now, not comfort, so she hung on tighter.

Rand was being strangled. He tried to keep his eye on Kerry, trailing after them, carrying her own bag and the little paper bag of possessions. He'd help her after he got Danielle calmed down. Right now he needed to get this whole caravan on the correct bus.

Ah! There it was.

He pressed on through the ever-present crowd, almost losing Kerry in the process. He reached back and grabbed her hand. "Hold onto the back of my shirt and do not let go. Keep your bag and purse in front of you to avoid pickpockets in the crowd."

Kerry grabbed the loose cloth of his shirt in the back, twisting a fistful tightly in her grip. She almost tore it when several people threatened to overwhelm her, pushing to get up the bus steps.

Once inside the bus, there were no seats to be had. Rand walked to the back, turned around, and squatted with another older man in the aisle. Kerry just looked at them and wondered what she should do.

"Squat down, Miss Carlyle, and go native," Rand said with half a grin.

"Excuse me, I'd rather stand," Kerry replied and turned around to see if there was a place up front.

"You'll be sorry," was the last thing that Kerry heard.

The bus lurched forward, and Kerry slammed backward and sat down hard. She quickly looked around, but Rand was pointedly looking the other way. However, Danielle was giggling at her, and it was almost worth the fall and the embarrassment to see the child smile. Kerry smiled back and crossed her eyes.

That made Danielle giggle again. Kerry smiled sweetly, with the most wide-eyed, innocent face possible, when Rand looked at her.

He knew he had missed something just from the incredibly angelic expression she was casting on him. He was pleased that Kerry had not chosen that awkward moment to throw a tantrum over the lack of traveling amenities. He'd wait to tell her that these were upscale accommodations, even if they were on the floor.

"How are you doing, Danielle?" Rand asked, relieved that she'd relaxed her grip around his neck.

Instead of answering his question, Danielle looked seriously in his eyes and asked, "We are going to get

Kathryn now, aren't we?"

"Yes, she's at your bungalow with your *ayah*."

"Good, she's probably wondering where we all went. She might be scared."

Kerry caught Rand's eyes above the blond head. He looked at her as they both wondered about the delusions.

The bus traveled through New Delhi, stopping often, and finally Kerry and Rand were able to get seats. Eventually Rand got Danielle to sit beside him, instead of on his lap, with one bandaged hand stuck in the crook of his arm.

Finally, the three alighted in front of a walled compound that had an armed private guard standing at the gate.

Rand now shouldered Kerry's carry-on. She was feeling a little better about Rand's presence as he spoke to the guard in Hindi. They walked in, Danielle darting away and running to a small bungalow. A curly-haired child was playing in the front yard. When Danielle saw her sister, she started calling, "Kitty, Kitty, Kitty!"

The much younger child heard her nickname. She looked up, and her eyes got very big when she saw her sister. They grabbed each other and danced around together. Kathryn, only four, would not let go of her older sister and finally burst into tears. That brought the *ayah* out of the house, and she also started crying when she saw Danielle with those big bandages on her arms.

Rand and Kerry stood at the gate of the yard, watching the affectionate, if soggy, reunion and feeling a little left out of the homecoming.

Rand cleared his throat, "What have you got in this hideous pink bag? It's very heavy."

Kerry smiled and said, "Everything I thought might be useful." Except the poison for your coffee, thank you very much.

Rand shifted the carry-on around to the other shoulder, not realizing that he had dislodged the envelopes in his pocket.

Kerry bent to pick them up and pass them back, but the pasted letters caught her eye. With no thought for Rand's privacy, she read them and blurted out, "You're being threatened!"

"Hey! Give those to me," Rand made a grab, but Kerry was quicker. An old habit resurrected itself from her days of sibling skirmishes, and she held them behind her back.

"Who sent these?"

"I don't think they want me to know. That's why they keep pasting those little letters together to make their words," Rand shot back.

"Don't be smart with me. I meant, do you have an idea who's sending them?"

"I think I have some competition in my neighborhood with the local Hindu *mahant*, or leader. He occasionally stops by the school, where I do some small surgeries, ranting and raving. But I'm pretty sure he can't read or write English, a necessary skill to send these little love notes."

"Can't you do anything to stop him?"

"I don't really know that it is him, but thank you for your valued opinion, Miss Carlyle."

Both turned back stiffly to the yard and saw three pairs of wide eyes watching them intently.

Rand spoke to the *ayah*, who looked to be about fifteen years old, introducing himself in Hindi.

"I speak English, sir, because my sister teaches. My name is Koshoualya, but please call me Koshou," she said, opening the gate. Her name sounded like "co-shoe" to Kerry.

Kerry introduced herself, and the four females moved into the house in a large chattering bunch, leaving Rand behind, literally holding the bag.

After they were inside, Rand protested to a small lizard on the walk, saying, "No, no, ladies, don't wait for me."

He could see the burnt lab in the back and decided to look a little closer. He walked around the house to the black hole and burnt shell left by the explosion. The back yard was small, with a waist-high wall surrounding it. Everything in the lab had been destroyed. Nothing recognizable was left.

Rand walked around the garden. Many of the shrubs and trees had been trampled in the effort to put out the fire. As he walked around the bushes, at the rear of the garden he spotted something shiny in the shrubs. He parted the greenery and saw a man's watch. He picked it up. It was still ticking, and it was American made. He wondered how it had survived the explosion and fire. The crystal wasn't even cracked.

Now it seemed second nature to look for more shiny things in the grass. On the other side of some tall plants, he found a man's wedding ring, and by the stone wall, separating the yard from the alley, he found an expensive ball-point pen. All the items looked fairly new, in good shape and not very worn.

"What on earth am I finding?" he asked himself. Perhaps these things belonged to a typical absentminded professor who was always losing personal articles. Or they might have been thrown clear of the explosion, if they were left on a lawn chair or window ledge.

Rand thought of asking Danielle if the items were her father's, but he was afraid of upsetting her, increasing her delusions, and being wrong. Instead, he went into the house and called Koshou onto the side verandah. He spoke in Hindi so that Kerry and the girls wouldn't happen to overhear. "Have you seen these before?"

"Oh, yes, the watch and ring belong to Mr. Gunderson. He wore them always. The pen might be his. He liked that kind."

"He hadn't lost them lately?"

"I never saw him take them off. The watch was waterproof, and his daughters thought that was funny because he wore it swimming."

Koshou continued with another thought. "Dr. Dennison, when I stay overnight with Kathryn, here at the house, my father sends my younger brothers to stay with us. One brother thinks someone is watching this house at night. I did not tell Mrs. Dennison or the children."

"She is not Mrs. Dennison!"

Koshou smiled when he turned around.

Rand walked into the main part of the house, saw Danielle and Kathryn playing in their room, saw the suitcases Koshou was packing for them, but didn't see Kerry anywhere. "Danielle, where is Miss Carlyle?" he asked.

Both girls held fingers to their lips with an exaggerated "shhhhhh!" They giggled behind their hands and pointed to one of the twin beds in the room. It was a mountain of dolls and stuffed animals.

"That's nice," he said with exaggerated patience.

"Now, where is Miss Carlyle?"

"Look!" Danielle said emphatically, pointing to the bed again. Kathryn sat down on it and proceeded to comb one of the doll's hair. Rand stepped closer and then realized that, hidden under dolls, animals, and a blanket, was Kerry, curled on her side, out like a light. Kathryn was in fact, combing her hair, not a doll's.

"Uh, oh. Looks like the jet lag caught up with her. I forgot all about it. I'm sure you girls won't disturb her. I'll see if Koshou can make us a little snack."

Surprisingly, Rand reached down and gently pulled off Kerry's shoes, placing them next to the bed. Kathryn again gave him a big "shhhhhh" sign, and he solemnly returned it, nodding his head in agreement.

He headed into Mr. Gunderson's home office, after checking with Koshou on the availability of a snack. He couldn't help but wonder if there were any clues to the identity of the people who had destroyed the lab. On the desk sat a family photo, Danielle with one arm around her dad's neck and Kathryn sitting with her mom. Rand didn't know them, and yet he felt his throat tighten. The children's loss seemed more personal now that he had seen them as a family unit.

He rifled through everyday bills, personal notes, and other business correspondence but couldn't find anything that seemed unusual.

"Am I imagining some importance to these items?" he wondered aloud. "I can't figure out my own problems, but I think I'll play Sherlock Holmes and pick up hints from the garden and put it all together. Just drop it, Rand," he said, talking to himself, as he often did. It was a bad sign, he thought. Pretty soon he'd have twenty-seven personalities,

41

all designed to keep him from being lonely.

"Dr. Dennison, you wanted me?" Koshou asked, flour up to her elbows.

"No, no, I'm just talking to myself. What are you making?"

"Some *puris* and *sambar*, yes?"

"Yes, yes, yes. I am very hungry. Call me and wake Miss Carlyle when you are ready."

Rand's day had started very early with a clinic, some small surgery, work on the Bible school roof, and finally this business with Miss Carlyle and the children. It only caught up with him when he sat still. Rand put his head down on the desk, just to close his eyes for a minute, and went to sleep.

Koshou quietly called Danielle and Kathryn from their room. "Shhhh. We will go to the market while they nap. I will let each of you choose your own sweet if you hurry and get on your shoes."

The girls always considered this a treat, for they loved the market. Kathryn was more shy and kept one hand firmly gripped onto part of Koshou's sari, peeking out at all the brightly colored fruits, materials, and brass. Danielle, old enough to have a little spending money, was learning to dicker in Hindi.

They quietly left the house, walking the four blocks with ease in the bright sunshine. Koshou looked at fruit and eventually bought a small watermelon. Then she went on to the vegetables and got some fresh tomatoes to add to their meal. At one of the last vendors, she and the girls decided on sweets.

Koshou was just paying for them when Kathryn cried, "Mommy!" and started to run after a group of women.

Koshou threw the money at the vendor while she and Danielle followed in hot pursuit. If they lost sight of the little girl here, she could be picked up in a wink. There was little safety for a child running alone in the market.

Koshou, fortunately young and in good shape, quickly gained on Kathryn. She grabbed the hysterical child, who was pointing and screaming, "Mommy, mommy!" at a group of orthodox Muslim ladies, distinctive in the *burkhas* they wear, which are full-length heavy veils that leave only the eyes of the woman exposed.

Danielle did not stop at Koshou and Kathryn. She kept on running and caught up with the group, who now had turned to see who was running after them. They were all Indians, with eyes heavily lined in kohl. The small amount of their skin that was exposed was dark, not light.

Danielle walked slowly back to where Koshou was squatting down, trying to comfort the weeping Kathryn.

"Did she see a white lady?" Koshou asked.

"I don't know. I didn't see one anywhere."

Finally, Koshou passed her market bag, made from string, to Danielle and picked Kathryn up, carrying the still crying child home. They made quite an entrance.

Kerry rushed into the living area, confused from her deep sleep. Rand came booming in, ready to vanquish any villains, while Kathryn just kept crying and howling.

Danielle wound up explaining while Koshou took her sister into the other room and rocked her to sleep.

Rand looked very intently at Danielle and asked, "Did you get a good look at those women?"

"They looked like regular housewives going to market. My mom wasn't one of them. Believe me, I checked."

"You did very well. Thank you, Danielle. You'd better

check the food; it may need stirring."

When she was out of the room he looked at Kerry, "What do you think?"

"She must have seen someone that reminded her of her mom. She's so little and probably is not able to understand about death. Perhaps seeing her sister after a few days' absence made her assume she'd also see her parents. It makes me feel dreadful for the darlings."

"Go ahead and eat with Danielle, and I will make some phone calls from the office here. Have Koshou bring in a tray for me. Get some things for the children to have overnight, and I'll make arrangements for you to come back tomorrow to do some serious packing. By then, the jet lag will be a little better, although I expect your internal clock will be all mixed up for the next day or so."

Rand stepped back into the office, closed the door, and started the laborious process of calling the police and the morgue. There was no such thing as a simple phone call in India. It was always a study in patience.

Kerry looked in on sleeping Kathryn, her blanket tucked under her head and held in a death grip. Tears left tracks down each cheek. Kerry brushed back a damp curl on the sleeping child's face, and then she went into the kitchen.

Danielle sat at the table while Koshou cooked something on a ring set above a kerosene burner. There was no stove such as Kerry was used to. The burner and ring sat on a spotless floor. Koshou squatted beside it and looked far more comfortable and at ease than the typical American woman who did all her cooking standing up.

An American stove with little depressions, collecting spatters every time you cooked, was far more complicated to clean. Koshou simply moved everything and swept the floor. Kerry had always hated to clean the burner pans, and this intrigued her to no end.

"What are you cooking?"

"*Sambar*, or peas cooked with spices."

Kerry just nodded, not having any idea what kind of peas or spices to expect.

"We will have a cooking lesson, yes?" Koshou asked delightedly, much like any American teenager who finally gets to teach an adult something.

"O.K."

She watched as Koshou smiled and explained, stirring the *sambar* and throwing in handfuls of coconut, cumin seeds, coriander seeds, ground cinnamon, tamarind, hot chili powder, garlic, and brown sugar. The peas turned out to be black-eyed peas.

"I will soon go to the university and become a teacher like my sister."

"Your English is wonderful. You will be a very good teacher, I'm sure."

Koshou made a simple dough of whole wheat flour, some oil, and a little water and salt. It was stiff but smooth, and she rolled it into a long snake. Then, pinching off one inch at a time, she used a short, fat rolling pin to roll each piece into a medallion shape. Taking the *sambar* off the ring, she put on a shallow frying pan holding a little oil. When she put each dough medallion in, it puffed like a little pillow! These were the *puris*.

When Kerry sat down next to Danielle, she was served on a small aluminum platter called a *thali*. There was a separate aluminum container of yogurt sauce, called *raita*, which contained grated scallions, green chilies, paprika, and cucumber.

"Do you pray before you eat, Danielle?" Kerry inquired.

"Of course," the child replied matter-of-factly.

"Well, would you pray for our meal before we eat, please?" Kerry prompted.

Koshou must not be a Christian, Kerry guessed, because she watched with great, open curiosity.

Danielle closed her eyes and prayed with earnestness. "Dear God, thanks for the food, but I really wish you'd get my parents back. Love, Danielle."

Kerry thought it a most unusual, but nice prayer. She looked for a fork or spoon. She was almost ready to ask when Danielle elbowed her and pantomimed with her fingers. Apparently, utensils were not needed.

Kerry gamely tried, putting three fingers together like a scoop. The taste was heavenly.

"Danielle, quit tickling my leg with your toes."

Danielle looked at her quizzically.

"I can feel your little foot tickling the back of my leg, silly. You can't fool me," Kerry said smiling, amused that the little girl thought to scare her.

Danielle pointed to her lap, and Kerry could see both of her feet because she was sitting cross-legged on her chair.

Suddenly she sat very, very still. She could still feel it.

"Danielle? Koshou?" she whispered, "What is on my leg?"

# FOUR

**KERRY WAS AFRAID** to look.

Danielle made a funny chirping sound and snapped her fingers. A purple-faced monkey crawled into her lap from under Kerry's chair.

"I am sorry, but Bubbles doesn't have very good manners. She loves to tickle visitors with her tail."

"Will she bite?"

"Oh, no. My father bought her from one of the villages far from the city. She was supposed to be their supper, and she had a wire around her neck that was cutting into the skin. Dad clipped the wire, and then Bubbles, who was still a baby, climbed into his jacket and would not come out. She held on tight and came right on home with him. Dad had to pay for the family's meal, of course."

"I've never seen a monkey like her before."

And indeed, Bubbles was an unusual monkey. She was about two feet tall but skinny with a long, curling tail of at least a yard. Her fur was black, and her head wore a brown crown with long, white whiskers. The naked skin of her face was bright purple.

"Mr. Gunderson bought a *kasi-johni*," Koshou added.

"They are highly sought for their meat and pelt by non-Hindu tribal people."

"I thought monkeys were sacred in India," Kerry asked, perplexed.

"A good Hindu will not spill any animal's blood, although some Hindus eat meat. But the only sacred monkeys are the great ones such as the langurs."

Kerry didn't think she'd be bothering any monkeys, sacred or not.

Danielle had some information to share on the subject. "The langurs are mean and nasty tempered. They steal from houses and shops, but people just laugh at them and leave them alone. My dad told me to avoid them and to keep Bubbles out of their way because they might bite her."

Bubbles chose that moment to take a small piece of fruit from Danielle's plate. Koshou came screeching and waving a spoon when she saw it, and the purple-faced thief judiciously scampered out the window.

"Do not let him near your food! He may eat from the garden, but do not let him touch your plate. Do you understand? I must get you another one now."

Danielle giggled and nodded, not very intimidated by this lecture. "In Koshou's family, it is against caste for anyone else to touch someone's food after it is served, let alone a monkey. I don't mind, but she can't stand it," Danielle explained to Kerry.

Kerry wondered how caste was broken. She knew that Indians were born into a caste, or certain level of society, but hadn't known about the various rules related to the caste system.

Kerry started to take a drink from her aluminum cup

and realized that she wasn't supposed to drink anything that wasn't bottled.

Koshou seemed to read her mind. "Mrs. Gunderson was somewhat worried about the children getting microbes, for which they have no tolerance, in the house water, so she built a water purifier. It chemically treats the water and should be all right for you."

Sure enough, in the corner of the kitchen stood an odd-looking apparatus that Koshou pointed to as she spoke. Well, Mrs. Gunderson was a biochemist; she should know. Kerry took a big drink. It tasted heavenly.

Rand walked in, carrying an empty *thali*, evidence that he had eaten in the study while trying to make phone calls. "Thank you, Koshou; that was delicious! Miss Carlyle, may I speak with you one moment?"

Kerry followed him into the study and sat down in a chair next to the desk.

"I have just finished speaking with the local police," he began, "and they have given me the extraordinary information that they cannot find any human remains in the explosion debris."

"You mean they were burned to dust?"

"No, even the hottest kiln leaves residue, and this was not a controlled experiment. It means that either the Gundersons were not in that explosion, or else someone disposed of the evidence. Perhaps the police inadvertently mixed up the evidence with Koshou's dinner scraps. I want to believe the first, but my experience argues for the last scenario."

"Oh . . . to think that they might be alive! It would be so wonderful!"

"Maybe not. The police want to know if there was any

reason for the Gundersons to abandon their children and destroy the lab."

"You can't be serious? Who would abandon these precious girls?"

"It's interesting that you would mention that, because the police are wondering if the Gundersons might try and get the children before they leave the area."

"I do not believe this!" Kerry exclaimed. "What about Danielle's story, that bad men took her parents?"

"It is possible that Danielle was prepared for their disappearance or misinterpreted what she saw. And now I am extremely curious to know exactly what she saw," Rand said grimly.

They decided to wait and ask Danielle during a relaxed activity, in hopes of getting a more natural flow of remembrance.

A jeep arrived, sent from Rand's school. He and Kerry loaded it with the bags that Koshou packed and toys for the children from their room. Finally, with Danielle holding the monkey and Kerry holding Kathryn, they left the Gundersons' house with the promise to meet Koshou there the next morning for cleaning and packing.

They didn't have far to go and soon arrived in an older neighborhood with large homes.

"This area was built by successful industrialists but has fallen on hard times. I was able to help the school buy a property, but you will see that it needs much work," Rand explained as they pulled up in a small courtyard and saw a once grand house that looked as though it was falling apart.

The building rose three stories, an oddity in the area, where heat rises and makes top floors like saunas. A wide verandah circled the whole structure, and every doorway and window was wide open. Many young men and women seemed to be flowing in and out and around the place.

"We will be staying at the neighbors?" Kerry asked, wondering how long students waited for a rest room with all that competition.

"Yes, in fact, I will just drive over," Rand answered as he walked around the jeep, taking the driver's spot.

The home next door was not as large as the school but in far better condition. They drove into the courtyard, and a beautiful, tall blond woman came hurrying toward them from the house.

She wore a light safari jacket over long culottes and had beautiful hand-tooled sandals on her feet. Her hair was the palest blond, pulled back into a silk scarf. She looked cool, bathed, and delightful, which made Kerry feel like a grimy wretch.

Kerry's dress, "which would never wrinkle," was limp and damp from perspiration. Her feet, chafing inside the new, waterproof rubber sandals, almost slurped as she trudged along. She couldn't even get the sticky bits of hair away from her face because she was carrying the suddenly shy Kathryn.

"Hullo there!" Rand's neighbor called in a decidedly British voice. "You've finally arrived! Rand, I expected you hours ago."

Kerry watched Rand's reaction very closely. If he could live this close to the blond and not be in love with her, Kerry would eat her hat! Not that Kerry cared one smidgen, but she was always very observant.

"Gwen, thanks for waiting for us!" he said heartily as he strode over and shook her hand vigorously. He made introductions.

"Dr. Gwen Greyson, meet Kerry Carlyle, her charges, Danielle and Kathryn, and last but not least, Bubbles."

Rand unloaded the jeep, asking Kerry to be ready by seven in the morning for her ride back to the Gundersons' house. "We will have dinner at the school tomorrow evening when you're all finished," he added.

Kerry turned to Gwen, only to find that Bubbles, the traitor, was smitten. She was sitting next to Gwen's leg, her tail possessively wrapped around Gwen's ankle.

"You know I'm a doctor, Danielle, so I have unlimited curiosity about bandages. Do you think I could look under yours when it's time to change them tonight?" Gwen asked.

Danielle immediately puffed up with importance and pride in her bandages, readily agreeing. Even Kathryn got over her shyness and followed Gwen into the house.

Kerry sighed. Feeling like dirt and resembling the same, she picked up her bags and followed them all into the house.

"Well, I know Rand means well," Gwen began, "but we must find some way to get you out of that dinner invitation."

I just bet, Kerry thought.

Gwen continued, "His cook at the school is the worst. I'm fairly used to the village food, but even I cannot swallow his stuff. He's a volunteer, of course, so Rand can't do a thing about it. Are you hungry now, or would you prefer to get settled and bathed first?"

Kerry almost swooned at the thought of a bath. Could it be? "Well, we had a small snack at the bungalow, so I think we could wait."

Just then a round, middle-aged woman, all rosy

cheeked and smelling of lavender, came hustling out of the kitchen. "Oh, just look at the wee ones. Aren't you just sublime!" she cried as she hugged Danielle, Kathryn, and Bubbles in one swoop.

Gwen dryly said, "Mrs. Peters, one of them is a monkey. Miss Carlyle, meet my nanny and now tyrant dictator, Mrs. Peters." There was clearly great affection between Mrs. Peters and Gwen.

"Oh, it's lovely to meet you," Mrs. Peters began, in a slight Scottish brogue. "And it's a good thing that I just made some sugar cookies. Come into the kitchen, and tell me all about yourselves while I frost them. You don't like sugar cookies, do you?"

Two little faces solemnly nodded, and Kerry thought the monkey was almost smiling. "Mrs. Peters, this is so thoughtful. Would I have a chance to get freshened up while they're with you?"

"I would love it!" she answered enthusiastically. "I don't get a chance to fuss over little ones very often anymore. Of course, if Gwen would get married and have some . . ." She trailed off with a meaningful look toward Dr. Greyson.

"Oh, Mrs. Peters, I don't have any time," Gwen laughed in good humor, obviously used to the broad hints.

Kerry had heard that same excuse just hours ago with Rand. It sounded well rehearsed to her, from both parties.

Forty-five minutes later, hair washed, cool, and clean in fresh clothes, Kerry felt like a human being again. She wandered into the kitchen to find Mrs. Peters elbow deep in preparing dinner. Danielle and Kathryn were "helping," Mrs. Peters supplying them with exotic kitchen finery such as garlic presses, tea balls, and several bowls.

"Oh, Miss Carlyle, you look much revived and very pretty," Mrs. Peters smiled. "You can see that we are *all* making an elegant dinner for tonight."

Just then, the door to the dining room opened and an extremely handsome man stuck his head around it. He had silver-streaked hair, large shoulders, and an exquisite shirt, tie and jacket, from what Kerry could glimpse. He seemed to be in his early fifties, if she was any judge. He did not see Kerry or the children.

"Mrs. Peters, the aromas are making my mouth water. I will surely not make it until dinner. May I have a taste?" His British accent matched Gwen's.

"Ah, but you're a naughty one!" Mrs. Peters giggled, passing him a small plate that she obviously had already prepared. "Have you met Rand and Miss Gwen's friend, Mr. Greyson?"

He stepped into the kitchen then, and his eyes grew wide as he caught sight of Kerry, her drying hair loose to the waist, her face clean, soft, and finally cool.

"This?" he asked incredulously. "This is Miss Carlyle, the career woman from Geraghty and Miller? You are far too exquisite, my dear. I am Gwen's father, Tyler Greyson, but please call me Tyler."

Kerry felt less gawky, less cross, and a lot better. That British accent would have made directions to the grocery store sound elegant and romantic.

"Has anyone shown you the grounds?" he asked, still cradling her hand in both of his own.

"No."

Tyler tucked the hand into the crook of his arm and said, "Well, we have just enough time before dinner."

They walked around his lovely gardens and then farther

on the property.

"I own one of the shoe factories in New Delhi and some other little things. But the shoe factory is right on this property, behind the old stable in that long building. We will have to see it one day. If we go now, I'm afraid we would just be in the way, because everyone gets off in a few minutes. But I have a surprise for you in the old stable."

Tyler's easy banter and polished manners were easy on Kerry's rattled nerves. It was lovely to get away from the antagonism Rand seemed to provoke. Kerry wondered why he was so quick to get rid of her at the Greysons', avoiding all of them till tomorrow. Well, if Gwen didn't make it for supper, she'd know what was up. Not that she cared at all for Rand's company, especially with such an elegant companion.

"Do you agree?" the elegant companion asked, a quizzical expression on his face. Kerry realized with a start that she hadn't a clue as to what he had been talking about. Well, it probably wouldn't be anything terribly deep, so she decided to fake it.

"I'm not sure I understand. Do tell me some more."

"Well, most people think of elephants when they think of India, and I guess I couldn't resist the opportunity."

Kerry could have groaned in frustration. What was he talking about? For that matter, what was she talking about?

They reached the stables, which looked as though they had been built a long time ago. Tyler opened up a side door and motioned Kerry in. Her eyes took a few minutes to adjust to the darkness, and then she saw it. An elephant was standing in a big pile of straw.

"It's wonderful!"

Tyler positively beamed. "I bought her when I heard that the Gundersons' children were coming. I want the children to name her."

"Tyler, how thoughtful of you! The girls will be ecstatic. How did you know their last name?"

He looked blank for a moment and then smiled. "Rand must have mentioned it. The elephant's trainer is at dinner now, but we will bring the children over tomorrow. Don't tell them about my secret. I want to see their faces."

The rest of the evening passed enjoyably, with a superb dinner and Dr. Gwen entertaining them with stories about her trips to the villages around the city, giving immunization clinics, and teaching hygiene and first aid.

Then Tyler had some questions for Kerry. "Do I understand correctly that you and Rand are part of the same church organization?

"Well, my father is a minister and pastor, and I guess he recently met Rand's father, a former missionary, at a missions conference. The two must have exchanged information," Kerry shrugged.

Gwen's eyebrows rose as she said, "I thought you might also be involved with the Bible school project. We've had quite a few young, single American ladies come to volunteer their time here."

"Bible school? Rand didn't say it was a Bible school. He said he was establishing a clinic at a school."

"Oh, he is," Gwen added knowingly, "but he is also very dedicated to his religion and is establishing a place to train ministers. I, of course, am only involved in the clinic."

Kerry wondered at all this new information. Visitor's visa, my foot, Dr. Rand Dennison.

Tyler broke in, "But we occasionally go to the Bible school's special services. I love the people!"

Gwen smiled at her father indulgently. "Yes, Dad loves the students."

Now, there is one tough cookie, Kerry thought as she watched Gwen give her father the same stiff smile that Kerry reserved for her own folks when they acted unsophisticated.

It occurred to Kerry that she had never really answered the question of whether or not she was part of a church organization. She certainly never thought of herself that way when she was on business. On the other hand, she didn't really consider herself lacking religion, with a father who was a pastor. Well, no need to bring it back up.

Mrs. Peters assumed a lot of the care of Danielle and Kathryn, and when Kerry protested, Gwen and Tyler assured her that Mrs. Peters loved small children. And indeed, the girls seemed completely at ease with the former nanny. They ate in the kitchen while the adults had their meal.

Mrs. Peters bathed, scrubbed, shampooed, and dressed them in the new nightgowns that Kerry left on their beds. Gwen excused herself for a few minutes to rewrap the bandages on Danielle's arms.

When she came back, she was smiling. "There's no sign of infection, and they're healing nicely. We should start exposing them to air, without the bandages, in a day or two."

During dessert, Mrs. Peters brought the two small girls in and pushed them forward to give the adults good night kisses. Kerry could well believe that she was a very fine nanny.

They looked like shiny angels as Gwen leaned one cheek down for her kisses. Tyler put one girl on each knee and hugged them both, looking very pleased.

"Oh, I miss having sweet little girl kisses," he said and truly seemed to mean it. "I wish you lived here all the time!"

Both girls enthusiastically hugged him back, and Kerry thought how much they needed a daddy.

For her turn, both said polite thank-you's for the nighties, obviously coached from the sidelines by Mrs. Peters. Then they hugged Kerry, and Danielle whispered in her ear, "Can we sleep with you tonight?"

Kerry felt much warmed by the compliment. Her room adjoined the old nursery and she whispered back, "I'll come get you when I go up to bed later on."

And she did. Mrs. Peters found all three of them, sleeping soundly in Kerry's double bed, when she brought up a tea tray the next morning.

They hurriedly dressed, and Kerry was able to comb Danielle's hair now that Mrs. Peters had dealt with it. The previous evening, the older woman had washed it and rinsed it with lemon juice, then held Danielle on her ample lap, singing while she carefully brushed out every snarl with an old horse-currying brush. Danielle hadn't objected once, because Mrs. Peters was so gentle.

The jeep, with yet another driver from the school, was parked outside, and because they didn't have time to sit down for breakfast, Kerry and the children grabbed big banana muffins to eat on the way.

Pulling up at the Gundersons' bungalow, they saw Koshou sitting on the steps, her head in her hands, looking dejected.

"Are we late?" Kerry called out before she even got out of the jeep. But Koshou did not respond.

When they reached her, she simply looked at them in a daze, tears running down her face.

Kerry rushed into the house and stopped cold.

# FIVE

**KERRY STOPPED ABRUPTLY,** and Danielle careened into the back of her. The house was empty. Completely empty! There was not one piece of furniture, one item of personal property, one scrap of paper, or one paper clip left. Whoever had come in and burglarized the bungalow overnight had left only the kitchen intact. Everything else had vanished.

It made Kerry feel violated and angry, and this wasn't even her property.

Danielle stood very still with huge tears tumbling out of her eyes. Kathryn did the most therapeutic thing and crawled into Koshou's lap, wrapping her arms around the weeping *ayah*.

"Those bad men did this," Danielle said brokenly.

"Yes, some very bad men did this," Kerry comforted, patting and hugging the child.

"No!" Danielle responded vehemently, "Not some bad men, the same bad men that took my parents. How come no one believes me?"

The horrors of the past week seemed to visit Danielle anew. Kerry put her arms around the child and let her cry

61

and cry into her soft shoulder, until finally, with great shaky breaths and much gulping, she stopped long enough to hear the comforting words that Kerry was whispering over and over.

"Oh, I'm so sorry, Danielle. It's all so unfair. I'll listen, I promise. Just tell me and I'll listen."

Danielle paused, her eyes closed and her forehead leaning against Kerry's shoulder, and then she began.

"My sister, Koshou, and I were in the front yard playing ring toss when a big boom came from the lab. We all ran and saw a big fire where the lab had been. I knew my parents were working in there, so I tried to run in, but the gardener grabbed me and held me by the rear wall of the back garden. He held my head over his shoulder, so I wouldn't watch the fire, but I could see into our neighbor's yard and through to the road. A car was parked on the road and an Indian was climbing in, pushing a man's head down to get in before him. I think it was my dad. My mom might have been in there too."

She took a big breath and continued. "The Indian climbed in quickly and the car took off fast. When I tried to tell the gardener, he passed me to the police, who thought I was upset. They let a nurse and then a doctor look at me, but no one has believed a word that I've said."

Kerry did believe the little girl; she just wasn't sure if the child really saw her father or some other person in the car. "I know you're telling me the truth, Danielle. We will tell Rand when we get a chance, O.K.? Maybe he'll know how to make the police listen."

They shook hands on it.

Kerry calmed Koshou, promising to get in touch with her as soon as Kerry knew anything about the burglary.

Kerry then loaded Koshou into the jeep, instructing the driver to take her home and then come back for them. A police report would have to be filed, but Kerry didn't know how or who to call, so she'd consult with Rand first.

The jeep made its way back to the school, slowly maneuvering through the streets. Kerry held Kathryn on her lap, while Danielle leaned against her side. They were all very distressed.

The sky seemed to echo their mournful faces, growing dark and gray, as clouds covered the hot sun. Kerry was amazed to see a storm gather so quickly.

The previous night she had awakened in the middle of her sleep, the jet lag stirring her awake at 1:30 AM, New Delhi time. Of course, her body thought it was 3:00 in the afternoon, Ohio time. She'd wandered quietly around the room, afraid of waking the children.

At the window, she'd watched the moon and the clouds drifting over it. She could also see the school, which had lights shining from the ground floor. There were people awake over there, moving in and out of rooms. Kerry couldn't see them clearly, but she could see their shadows against the muslin curtains as quite a number of people walked around. What on earth were they doing?

Kerry slipped out of the upstairs bedroom and felt her way along the hall to the banister. She was very careful, feeling her way down the steps with tentative toes.

In the library she was able to get a closer look at the school. Yes, there were people moving around, and lots of them, too.

Kerry checked the library clock. It was 1:30 in the morning! Dr. Dennison was keeping some late hours.

Perhaps it was a party, although they weren't noisy enough to hear across the yard. No wonder he couldn't wait to unload them. He had something going on.

Kerry finally went into the kitchen, fixing a cold roast beef sandwich from dinner's leftovers and a hot cup of tea. With that fortification, she went back into the library. The phone sat there, and she decided to put a call through to her parents so that they would know she was all right and had arrived safely.

It took almost twelve minutes to get through to the United States. Kerry had no idea that that was record-breaking time for a call in India.

Her father accepted the charges. "Kerry? Are you all right?" he shouted, the connection bad.

"I'm fine, Dad. I got in and Dr. Dennison found me. We picked up the two little girls, and I'm staying with some of Dr. Dennison's neighbors, the Greysons. I'll give you their number in case you need to reach me." Kerry gave him the number.

"Kerry, I've also got Rand's number, in case I can't get you."

Oh, good, Kerry thought. "Hey, Dad, I'm not that impressed with Dr. Dennison."

"Why, Kerry, he's a . . ." The line had so much static, that Kerry couldn't hear what her dad said. His voice came through again. "We've been worried about you. But we prayed about it and God gave us a real peace about this trip you've taken. Don't forget, you're a child of the King. Your mother's at the store, but I'll tell her you called."

Kerry hung up and looked at the phone darkly. "Well, Dad, I'm real glad God gave you some peace about my trip. He's given me nothing but trouble since I got here!"

Kerry had moved away from home about three years ago, getting a job in the city. Since leaving her home town and her home church, where she was very actively involved in helping her parents, Kerry had drifted from congregation to congregation.

Some churches were so cold and others were so tiny that she had no friends her own age. And then her job required so much overtime that she was often too tired to attend on Sundays. All in all, it was easy to get out of the habit of regular church attendance. Her parents worried about it, she knew. Her father never missed an opportunity to bring it up.

Eventually, Kerry wandered back upstairs. By now it was almost 2:30 AM, and she was getting drowsy again. She checked the window and noted that there was still quite a bit of activity over at the school.

"I must ask someone about it tomorrow," she breathed as she moved the two little limp bodies over and climbed into bed.

Kerry remembered last night's events clearly now and sternly told herself to ask about the activity when they arrived at the school.

The jeep pulled into the front courtyard of the school, so that Kerry and the children could get out. They were walking toward the verandah when a tall man stepped from around the corner of the building.

He was naked, covered in ash, with hair that fell to his shoulders in long, twisted ropes. He swayed, not more than a foot in front of them and fell with a crash.

It was all too much. First the shock of finding the bungalow robbed and now this scary guy. All three females indulged in hysterical screaming, holding onto each other and howling at the top of their lungs.

The whole school came racing out, just as a deluge of rain started. Rand, coming from the topmost floor, arrived last and found Kerry and the children screeching, all the students running around, and a naked man passed out on his doorstep.

He had the very human urge to run back inside and bolt the door, but when he saw that there was no imminent danger, the whole thing struck him, quite suddenly, as funny. He had to bite his lip as he tried to put things in order.

First he stooped, checking the man's breathing, which seemed normal. "Pick this man up, take him to the infirmary, pray for him, and get Dr. Greyson," were orders he barked to two or three strong male students.

"Ladies, bring Miss Carlyle inside and get her some dry clothes. You two, come with me," he smiled as he picked up the children who needed someone calm to stabilize things. He carried them over to the Greysons' to Mrs. Peter's kitchen.

Danielle sobbed out the news about the burglary and her version of the lab fire as he carried them over. The rain quickly stopped because February was the beginning of the dry season, and rain showers were short when they did occur.

He nodded, obviously taking in all that Danielle said. "Danielle, I do not know what happened to your parents, but there are quite a few things that do not add up in this business. I will work on it, but I can't promise any results, O.K.?"

That was good enough for the drained child.

"Mrs. Peters, I have two wet, tired, pitiful children that I found in my front yard. It seems they've had a rough morning and are in desperate need of some dry clothes, lunch, and sweets. You wouldn't happen to have anything like that around?"

Rand left them in Mrs. Peters's warm hug. They were toweled off while they ate coconut cookies, and they told Mrs. Peters about their house and the naked man, giggling, which was better than being frightened.

The last thing Rand heard as he departed was Danielle's best "isn't it awful" voice saying, "And Mrs. Peters, he wasn't even wearing any underwear!" Rand was glad that Mrs. Peters was handling it.

Back at the school, Kerry was surrounded by chattering ladies, all in white blouses and blue skirts. They were whispering and moving her up the stairs to the ladies' dorm. They pushed her through the door and left, except for one beautiful student, who had the whitest, brightest smile Kerry had ever seen.

"I am Sister Minnie, the office secretary," she introduced herself. You are Sister . . . ?"

Kerry hesitated before answering. It had been a long time since anyone had addressed her as "Sister." Although it was a common custom to use that preface in her father's congregation, she had rarely practiced it, preferring to call her friends by their first names only. She reserved "Brother" or "Sister" for her parents' contemporaries, much like using the honorary "Uncle" or "Aunt."

On the other hand, she did not want Minnie to think she was prejudiced. "I'm Sister Kerry," she finally answered.

"I would like to assist and get you some more clothes,

yes?" she asked politely, her accented English very correct.

Kerry, dripping water, readily agreed. Looking down at her clothing, she turned bright red. It seemed that parachute silk, which never ever wrinkled, turned transparent when wet. Kerry groaned, hoping that the naked man had taken everyone's attention from the nearly naked lady!

It was suddenly apparent why all those ladies had clustered around her and moved as a flock of sparrows in unison. They'd been covering her up!

Minnie brought a big box from a closet. "Many kind people donate clothing. I have some saris that will adapt to your size," she added thoughtfully.

Kerry knew that she was quite tall and large compared to most petite Indian ladies.

Minnie pulled out a shirt, scoop necked and short sleeved, that Kerry pulled over her head after pulling off the wet clothes. It was rather tight and made Kerry feel a bit like a pin-up girl.

"Sister Kerry, that is the *choli*," Minnie patiently explained. "When I wrap the sari, I will wrap it so that you will be covered adequately."

She took a bright yellow length of material, almost nine yards long, with a small flower woven along the border. Folding three big pleats at one end, Minnie pressed the folds against Kerry's waist and had her hold it. Then she began to wrap, leaving a long walking stride for the American woman. Finally, she draped the material over Kerry's left shoulder and around like a shawl, covering her bosom.

Kerry grinned at her reflection in a small, round mirror on the wall. She combed out her wet hair, parted it in the middle, and braided it to her waist. It was pretty authentic, other than the auburn hair and green eyes.

Kerry shook her head and realized she'd gotten water in her ear. The cotton in her dress pocket was wet, too. She'd be lucky if her ear didn't get infected.

Just then Danielle and Kathryn wandered in, in dry play clothes, eating more cookies.

"Mrs. Peters said to tell you that we'll have lunch in about an hour, O.K.?" Danielle said through a mouthful of cookies. "What'cha doin'?"

Danielle's father may have been Swedish and her mother French, but Danielle was all American. Her slang could only come from an American school, even if it was in the middle of India.

Minnie answered, "We are having some dress-up fun; would you like me to fix you?"

Kathryn and Danielle thought this would be great, and Minnie and Kerry enjoyed putting them both in cast-off outfits. They looked like beggars but thought they were queens in the long saris.

Walking downstairs, Kerry ran into Gwen.

"So, you found a Naga?" Gwen said lightly.

"You mean that man?"

"Yes," Gwen explained. "Nagas are from the far northeastern part of India, called Nagaland. In the past they were well known for cannibalism and also their nakedness. I have seen pictures of the chief's houses, with many human skulls lined up, decorating them for prestige."

"How did he get here?" Kerry asked.

"There are many Hindus who are making the special

pilgrimage for the *maha kumbh mela* right now. You will get to see many sects and oddities from all over our subcontinent. Although, why a Naga would come to New Delhi, many days walk out of his way, I do not know. Also, I must admit, I thought they were tribals, not practicing Hindus."

"Is he all right?" Kerry inquired.

"Yes, he looks fine to me. I do not know why he passed out. Nagas, I've read, are usually quite hostile to others, but this one was very passive when I examined him, very clean, and had no vermin or pestilence. He is also in excellent physical health and has perfect teeth, surely an unusual thing considering the primitive conditions that Naga villages are known for. I do not really understand it. He's resting now."

"Should we be afraid of him?" Kerry wanted to avoid him whether he was dangerous or not.

"There is always risk involved in helping others, but that is for the adults to accept. I would keep the children away from him, just to be on the safe side and to avoid any more startling situations," Gwen smiled. "Have you seen any ascetics yet?"

"I'm not sure," Kerry replied cautiously, not sure what an ascetic was.

"They would certainly startle you if you saw them in the streets. They are *sadhus*, or Hindu holy men. Following the ancient discipline known as *tapas*, they take vows to adopt extreme and painful postures or positions to acquire spiritual power and favor. You may see men who have not moved their legs from one position in years, those limbs atrophied, withered and now useless. I find them very distressing, as a doctor, but they are usually not dangerous."

"You and Rand are both doctors. Do you both do the same thing?"

"No, I am a general practitioner, and he is a general surgeon. The villagers love him when he removes unsightly growths and tumors."

Kerry nodded her head, understanding but hardly able to credit such humanitarian efforts to that rude man. "If you are both doing work in the villages, who runs the school?"

"A minister of some national standing and many years of service oversees the daily operation."

Suddenly, the two heard a smashing sound in the front courtyard. Running out, they saw a broken beer bottle and a rag aflame on the bare dirt of the courtyard. Fortunately there was nothing around to burn, but from the looks of the piece of cloth burning, a homemade bomb had been thrown. It burned on its own gasoline and finally went out.

"What happened?" Kerry cried.

"Someone filled a bottle halfway with kerosene or gasoline, stuck in a rag, lit it, and threw it over the wall," Rand answered in back of her. He heard the crash and came to see that everyone was safe. "If they'd had the luck or aim to throw it into the jeep, we would have had a serious problem."

"But why do they want to do this?"

Gwen answered this time. "Because we are white and bring new ideas of medicine and religion to their community. We will always be suspect in their eyes," she ended bitterly and walked off.

"Also because we lessen their holy men's control over his group of followers. We teach that germs and disease cause sickness, not disobedience to the guru. My friends, the missionaries, teach the people to pray directly to one God, who is sympathetic to needs and requires no pain or sacrifices. All in all, we're considered pretty revolutionary in our ideas to the Hindus," Rand smiled dryly.

"Do they vandalize your school often?"

"Lately, we have become a very popular target. Where are Danielle and Kathryn?"

Kerry looked around but didn't see them. She called their names, but no one responded. Rand checked the school building.

Kerry could feel her heart race as she began to panic.

Rand came running back outside. "I cannot find them, and the Naga is gone! Go check the Greysons'. I'll look out back."

Kerry raced over to the house next door and flung herself through the front door. Checking upstairs, in the nursery and her room, Kerry found no one. Running downstairs, she heard a voice in the library. Ready to launch herself in, Kerry overheard one side of a conversation that stopped her in her tracks.

"I'm no kidnapper! I will not pay that amount, and I want to know where you are!"

# SIX

KERRY UNDERSTOOD, and only too well! She charged in, interrupting Tyler's phone conversation. "Where are the children?" she demanded, her fists clenched.

Tyler looked at her. He put his palm over the phone and asked quietly, "What children?"

"Danielle and Kathryn. Where are they?"

Again, Kerry observed the blank look as Tyler answered slowly, "I don't know; they were here a few minutes ago. I'll help you look."

He looked concerned but not excited, telling the phone party to call him later and hanging up. Kerry was beginning to think that she misinterpreted his end of the phone conversation.

Gwen walked in as Tyler clicked the phone into place. Kerry asked if she had seen the children, and Gwen said that she had seen them out in the herb garden about five minutes ago.

"There," Tyler said. "I'll join you and we will check on them. You shouldn't get so upset," he admonished lightly.

Feeling like a fool and embarrassed at suspecting

Tyler of kidnapping, Kerry made an extra effort to respond with interest to his conversation and let him put his arm around her shoulders in a reassuring gesture. They stood at the kitchen door, which opened out to the herb garden, and found five girls instead of two, sitting in a circle under a tree.

Each wore a scarf over her head like women at the market, and they were having a wonderful mud pie party.

Kerry and Tyler looked at each other and laughed delightedly, the tension releasing itself in the moment.

"Obviously all is well," said a flat voice behind them. As Kerry looked back to see Rand, grim faced, she realized Tyler's arm was still around her shoulders.

She felt awkward and then angry because she was certainly not going to defend herself to that pompous doctor, who was so critical of her every move. Nevertheless, she wished Tyler would drop his arm.

"Yes," Tyler answered smiling. "We found them, if we can figure out which children are ours."

Rand gave him a sour look, and even Kerry looked askance at his choice of words. Ours?

Rand deliberately stepped between Kerry and Tyler through the door and whistled once. Instantly, two figures ran to him, blue and green eyes sparkling out of dirty faces. He did not smile back. Calmly but with great seriousness Rand said, "Miss Carlyle and I have been searching for you. You did not tell any grownups where you went. We must have a lesson to remember the rules! Meet me in my office after dinner tonight, and we will decide on a punishment."

The girls solemnly nodded, knowing they had done wrong. Rand turned back around, stepped between Kerry and Tyler, and started to leave.

"Dr. Dennison?" Kerry called.

"Yes," he answered, turning around slowly.

"The Gundersons' house was robbed last night!"

Tyler looked at Kerry with great seriousness, while Rand made a dismissive gesture with his hand. "I know all about it already. Danielle told me. I've taken the liberty of calling the police. They'll want to get a statement, when they get around to it. That could mean today, and it might mean next week." With that he stomped out.

Before Kerry could say a word, Tyler was on one knee in front of the two juvenile delinquents. "Now, let's look on the bright side, kids. I've got an elephant, and we can all go see her if you want. Maybe take a ride on her?"

Oh, they just loved the idea, hugging Tyler, getting mud all over him, and running to get their three friends. Kerry was torn between letting them enjoy the day and scolding them herself for worrying her so much.

When Tyler stood up and looked at her, with a big smear of black under one eye and a small, muddy hand print on his back, she couldn't help grinning. "I haven't had this much fun in years," he smiled, taking her hand in his and pulling her along, the little ones running in a group around them. "I hope you'll call me Tyler and give me the honor of using your first name?" he asked.

"Certainly, Tyler."

Kerry considered this interesting, because she found it very natural to use Tyler's first name, while she carefully used Rand's full title when addressing him. She knew his first name, but he'd certainly never encouraged any familiarity. In fact, he called her "Miss Carlyle."

They walked to the rear of Tyler's property to the

stables and found a young boy working with the elephant.

"How old?" Kerry asked.

"Only eleven years old. She recently had her first calf, but it died."

"I meant the boy, Tyler."

"Oh, he's probably around twelve or thirteen."

"Shouldn't he be in school?"

Tyler shrugged. "His family needs him to work. I pay him so much per month. I also paid the family a set amount to bring him here to work with the elephant. That was his father I was just speaking to on the phone. They keep wanting more money."

So that explained the conversation, Kerry mused.

"Where does he live? I haven't seen him at the house."

"Why, he lives with the elephant. They're inseparable!" Tyler exclaimed.

"He lives in these old stables?"

"It is far nicer than the hut he comes from. Do not pity him; it will make him lazy. This will be a job for most of his life. Elephants have a long life span, up to sixty years. And once they're attached to a *mahout*, there is no point in breaking up the pair. There are legends of elephants who have died of heartbreak after their *mahout* was killed."

"Well, they do seem to be having fun," Kerry commented as she watched the young boy pick up a large, dried dung chip, the kind used for fuel, and toss it toward his charge. The elephant immediately picked it up off the ground with her trunk tip and chucked it back at him. He giggled uproariously, as did the children. Then he found half of a coconut hull and repeated the game of toss. The elephant's aim was much better than the boy's. Even though he ran and dodged, she popped it off the top of his head time after time.

"Elephant society is very social," Tyler went on, "tightly knit and completely matriarchal. It works because there are such strong bonds between the oldest cow and her female descendants. When young bulls reach the age of puberty, they are expelled from the family."

"She must be missing her calf, then."

"I think so. She seems to like children a lot."

Kerry watched as the boy helped the children pass small pieces of fresh coconut to the outstretched trunk. He was very gentle with all the little hands, and it was clear that he had taken care of small ones before.

Tyler continued, "This female will not be ready for any heavy work for another year, but by then I think I will have great use for her. I bought her from a traveling circus that had fallen on hard times. She's used to giving rides and such."

"I saw an elephant on the Grand Trunk Road yesterday."

"Really? Did you know that elephants need a lot of water, at least thirty gallons a day, to drink? They also need water for bathing and supplying mud for their skin."

"You have to bathe elephants?" Kerry thought in terms of putting one in a tub.

"Elephants have very delicate skin, in spite of the leathery look of it. Mud helps cool the animal while providing a sticky base for the cloud of sand and dust that the elephant blows all over itself to protect it from sun and insects. Besides, they love to play in their water holes."

"You have a water hole on your property?"

"Kerry, my dear, I have everything this elephant

needs, and what I don't have, I can buy."

"Oh." That was quite a statement, Kerry considered.

"Will the children be supervised?" Kerry asked, watching the elephant lift them onto her neck as carefully as any mother.

"They will be careful." Tyler added, "And I'll tell the boy to keep an eye on them. The water is not so high at this time of year." He shouted a few things to the boy who nodded and saluted. "Let's go look at my shoe factory," Tyler suggested.

Kerry nodded in agreement, and they walked across a wide lot to the factory. It was far behind the stables. They walked on a path beaten down between waist-high walls of grass.

"You also own this land?" Kerry asked.

"Well, part of it. Dr. Dennison's school owns most of it, if they can keep up their mortgage and payments."

"I wasn't aware that it was Dr. Dennison's school. I thought missionaries ran it."

"Oh they do, but he's the money that keeps them afloat. He says he wants to establish a charity clinic there with a portable surgery to go out to the villages, but that's a bit hard to swallow. If it's all charitable, how will they support themselves?"

Kerry found this new revelation about Dr. Dennison very interesting.

Tyler went on without interruption. "These 'helping' kinds of businesses are always on the brink of bankruptcy," he said unconcernedly.

They arrived at the factory and went inside. Kerry was almost overcome by the heat and smell. Men were stripped down to *dhotis*, linen wound around their hips, working in crowded conditions, with inadequate lighting. There was no ventilation to speak of. Tyler pulled her along to the end of the production lines and proudly showed her the beautiful handmade leather shoes. They looked very expensive.

"I buy the designs from Italy, get them made up here, and take them to Europe to sell in the high-fashion market. Each pair of shoes takes three days to make, with more than fifteen people working on each design. Then I sell them for two or three hundred dollars a pair," he told her proudly.

Kerry had heard about the cheap labor in Third World countries but always thought that meant in the fields. "How much do your employees make?" she asked.

"I pay the going rate for factories here in New Delhi. Plus, I let my workers take home discarded scraps of leather."

Kerry felt a little better, imagining these men making shoes for their families at home. On the other hand, none of them seemed to be wearing shoes. Perhaps it was because of the heat in there.

"They are all Muslims, of course," Tyler said. "They will only work with sheep and goat skin because pigs are taboo. Hindus would never spill blood of any animal or work with their unfinished hides. Untouchables might, but these Muslims can read and follow directions very well."

Tyler took her for a tour of his office in the warehouse. His secretary came and asked if he would check with the foreman while he was there. He left the room and Kerry wandered around, glancing at his desktop, when a piece of letterhead caught her eye. It was the Geraghty and Miller logo, where she worked!

She curiously turned it around and saw that it was the first page of a soil core report. She dealt with those all the time in their home office. She scanned it but quickly turned it around and moved away from the desk as she heard Tyler coming back, embarrassed to be caught reading something on someone else's desk.

"I'm sorry to have kept you waiting!" he smiled. "We'll go pick up the children now. You're beginning to look tired, and I'm afraid it is my fault," he said solicitously, patting her hand.

"Oh, look!" Kerry said, trying her hand at acting. "That looks like the logo of my company on your desk!"

Tyler's eyes darted to the report. "Why, yes it is. I thought you knew that your company has done work for me before."

"No, I don't handle international business as a rule," Kerry replied.

"Well, the city is always asking for verification that we're not polluting the soil," Tyler explained as he steered her out of the office.

They began to walk back to the stables.

"You know, you look quite stunning in that native outfit," he said, a shade too heartily.

Kerry had forgotten that she was wearing a sari instead of her normal Western clothing.

Tyler chuckled. "I almost mistook you for one of the help when you came bursting into the house this afternoon."

Kerry didn't want to talk about her error. She must have seemed loony, demanding to know where the children were.

Tyler didn't refer to that but continued with his own

train of thought. "I quite like it for a laugh, but I'd rather see you in something high fashion. I hope you'll let me take you and Gwen out for a fancy evening soon. I will be the envy of all my friends at the club. Will you?" he asked beseechingly.

Kerry had mixed feelings about accepting. On one hand, she had packed a simple black dress that was elegant, but on the other hand, she was enjoying the freedom and comfort of the sari so much that she wished she had a fancy one. However, the thought of one evening, free of worry, almost a vacation, was very appealing. She nodded in acceptance, smiling with gratitude for his thoughtfulness.

They collected Danielle and Kathryn, who had named the elephant Tiptoe, their linguistic equivalent to the animal's Indian name.

Tyler, Kerry, and the girls walked back toward the school building. Kerry wondered about the Naga that she and the girls had seen and who had disappeared. She also wanted to make sure that Rand was still expecting them for dinner at the school. And for heaven's sake, she must remember to ask someone what was going on there in the middle of the night!

The girls, who were already dirty from climbing on the elephant, begged to play a while longer in the garden. Kerry left them with Tyler, who said he was going to take a nap in the hammock, while she went to check on the evening plans at the school.

She found Sister Minnie in the office.

"Oh, Sister Kerry, praise the Lord!"

It was a standardized greeting, and Kerry found herself answering in kind. "Praise the Lord, Sister Minnie. I wondered if the Naga man ever came back."

"I don't know if that man was a naked Hindu or one of the tribal Nagas. They are different, you see," Sister Minnie explained.

"The naked Hindus are considered holy men. In religious zeal, they own nothing, not even clothing. They travel around living frugally on others' charity. This man may have passed out from thirst or a brief illness, but upon coming to consciousness his first goal would be to move on. I'm not really surprised at his strange behavior."

"Thank you. I wondered about him. Also, I noticed the lights on last night. I wondered if there was a problem." Kerry tried to sound more concerned than curious.

"Oh, that was an all-night prayer meeting," Sister Minnie smiled. "Brother Dennison is probably trying to catch up with a nap, if you're looking for him. He said he would be in his office by two o'clock, if you would try then."

Kerry was full of wonderment that a doctor found enough energy to attend an all-night prayer meeting. Kerry had attended a few of those back in her teenage years. She really hadn't thought about it in ages but was surprised to find she had pleasant memories of those prayer meetings. They had passed quickly, and she had been blessed!

. Kerry smiled to remember how earnest she had been. In fact, Kerry had been a sincere Christian all through high school, witnessing to her friends and bringing many of them to church.

When had that changed? Of course, she reasoned, she still loved God. She just didn't pray as much or as often.

Kerry walked back to the Greysons' home, checking

on the children. Mrs. Peters, back from her afternoon shopping, was spraying a hose over the two "piglets" in the garden. She said she would not even let them in her house because she wasn't sure who was really under that dirt. Both girls laughed with delight. It was hard to say who was having a better time, the children or Mrs. Peters, who kept asking where those little piglets were hiding, now that her girls were back.

Gwen came through the yard, calling out to them. "Mrs. Peters, you'd better get them into a soapy tub. Danielle's bandages look dirty and wet. I'll come and look at her arms in half an hour, and then we'll decide whether we should wrap them up again."

"I could do that, Mrs. Peters," Kerry hurriedly offered. She didn't want to take advantage of the wonderful lady's kindness.

"Oh, no, I've already drawn their bubble bath," Mrs. Peters said happily, while the girls cheered.

Kerry found the resilience of children amazing. What grown-ups could have such tragedy occur in their lives and still look forward to a bubble bath?

"By the way, has anyone seen Bubbles lately?" Kerry wondered.

Danielle knew. "She found a friend. We saw her by Tiptoe before we left. She likes the elephant's boy, too."

Kerry laughed at the idea that the boy belonged to the elephant instead of the other way around.

Mrs. Peters and the children went inside the house, leaving Kerry alone in the garden. Kerry didn't seem to be needed anywhere. The children were fine, the Gundersons' house had nothing to pack, and she still had days left before their flight back to the United States.

Maybe she would get to see some of India's tourist spots after all. She'd have to find out what her options were.

She wandered back to the school and into the hallway that had a classroom on either side. Classes were in session. The students looked intent, their Bibles open in front of them.

Kerry had read the Bible through one year. She had followed the B.R.E.A.D. program, which stood for "Bible Reading Enriches Any Day," and divided the whole thing into daily readings. It had been fun and quite an accomplishment.

Kerry frowned. It had been a long time ago. She didn't find much time to read the Bible anymore.

Kerry looked in Rand's office and was surprised to see a well-dressed, middle-aged Indian who looked like an official. "I am sorry to startle you," he said in excellent English.

"Do you know where Mr. Dennison is?" Kerry asked.

"He will be back in a moment. You are . . . ?"

"Miss Carlyle, just here for the week."

"And Miss Carlyle, what do you have to do with this school?"

For some unexplained reason, Kerry felt suddenly wary, as if his innocent question held some vast importance.

"Not very much. I'm staying next door," she answered vaguely.

"Do you know what Dr. Dennison does here?"

Oh, boy, oh, boy, oh, boy, Kerry thought, putting her anxiety into beautiful rhetoric. Oh, boy, oh, boy, oh, boy.

"I know he is visiting and seeing his boyhood home again. He has many friends," Kerry answered, while thinking, Visitors on visas do not hold clinics and start Bible schools.

The man smiled and nodded, "Yes, I can see that he does."

Kerry jumped as Rand came up behind her. "I see that you have met Mr. Hansa Rupa Das from the state department," Rand stated, nodding toward the official.

Kerry smiled stiffly.

"Mr. Rupa Das has had some complaints from the neighborhood and has been sent to check my status as a tourist. I was just telling him that we are all going out to dinner tonight. Will you wear that delightful outfit, Miss Carlyle?"

Kerry nodded and backed away, anxious to leave the men alone. She hoped Rand wasn't in any trouble.

Two dinner invitations in one day. She knew that Rand's new plans had been on the spur of the moment, but even still!

She started to grin, thinking that Rand Dennison and Tyler Greyson had each requested dinner and a different type of dress, as opposite in styles as their own personalities were to the other. This could be fun!

# SEVEN

AN HOUR LATER, Kerry changed her mind about this being fun. She was sitting on a bus, in the very back, bouncing over dirt roads and trying to keep from bouncing into Rand every time they hit a pothole or rut.

When Rand said they were going out for dinner, he meant all the students and he meant "out." They were heading for a small, rural village about two hours away. The missionaries would have a church service, and he would be looking at some patients. The women at the village would prepare a meal for everyone.

Kerry was glad that the children were spending the evening with Gwen. This was the roughest ride she'd ever had on a bus.

Rand decided to get the students out of the building after he found the latest threatening letter on his desk that afternoon. It read, "I know where you are, day and night."

Rand had closed his office door and knelt on the floor, placing the letter in front of him. Students who passed by could hear the prayer seeping from under the door. No one looked surprised. Rand was known to be a praying man who trusted God and delighted in praising Him.

However, Rand was trying very hard to relinquish his own will and control in this matter of the letters. "Wonderful Jesus, I thank You for these letters that threaten us," he forced himself to pray. "I worship You, because You do all things well, including the situation regarding these letters," he added, and his own words began to reassure him. "I know that You are good and watch Your own sheep as a loving shepherd. I thank You for including me. I thank You for watching this school."

The prayer started to flow freely, and Rand began to praise and worship God. His heart lightened, secure in the reassurance of God's power. Rand's own worries seemed trivial when he prayed and worshiped, for God always had a plan. It just took prayer to remind the heart, ease the mind, and relinquish control to God.

With a security that he had not had in days, Rand calmly greeted Mr. Hansa Rupa Das later that afternoon and answered questions from the state department with honesty.

Mr. Rupa Das did not seem to be upset by the answers, although he wrote everything down in a little book. In fact, his questions had less to do with Rand than the school, the property, and the neighborhood.

Rand made a copy of his medical license to give to the man and had been pleased to find Kerry in the office when he got back. That saved him a trip next door to invite her to the service that evening. He did not know if she would want to come. He was having difficulty deciding if she approved or disapproved of the Bible school. She said very little about God or church or even the clinic.

Rand wore his habitual jeans and light cotton shirt to go out to the village, not stopping his work long enough during the day to change before it was time to go.

"Sister Minnie," Rand called across the aisle, "did you pack anything to drink?"

"Oh, yes, Brother Dennison! Here is a bottle of soda for you and one for Sister Kerry."

Sister Minnie and Kerry sat across the aisle from Rand. Kerry carefully held onto the seat in front of her. She didn't want to invade Rand's space across the tiny aisle, even if this ride was like a roller coaster, bouncing her around.

"Sister Kerry?" Rand said, "I think I need to get into the habit of addressing you as such, if you will give me permission. It sounds so much warmer and nicer than 'Miss Carlyle,'" Rand smiled with a wicked gleam.

Kerry shot him a cool look. He was goading her and she knew it. But she kept her retort to herself. She wouldn't hurt Minnie's feelings for the world. These students were so . . . so . . . frustratingly sincere!

Sister Minnie started to hum a worshipful chorus. Others joined their voices to the melody. Kerry had a beautiful alto voice and joined in. All the students heard the addition and smiled at her, nodding with enthusiasm. Rand now added a harmony in his clear tenor, enjoying the mix of voices.

"Jesus is the rock in a weary land, a shelter in the time of storm," reflected his new peace about the threatening notes, and he was able to smile and relax with the students' singing. Soon, the students were singing another chorus with great enthusiasm, and the bus passengers were enjoying the music.

Kerry didn't notice, however. She was beginning to feel very queasy. "Hey!" she shouted above the racket of the bus and their singing. "I need to stop!"

"You want us to stop singing?" Rand shouted back incredulously.

"No, I need to stop. I don't feel well."

Sister Minnie looked very concerned and told Kerry, "The bus will not stop until we get there. If you make him stop, he will leave us, and we would have to wait for his return much, much later tonight."

Kerry absorbed this knowledge, and it seemed to heighten her level of nausea. She didn't know it, but her face was completely white, stiff with self-control. Rand took one look at her clammy skin, slight shudder, tight fists, and grasped the urgency of the situation.

He turned and spoke to one of the Bible students, who promptly took a lunch sack, dumped out its contents, and passed the empty paper bag to Rand. Rand held the bag out to Kerry, who grabbed it desperately and turned her back.

Just in time! Great tears rolled down her cheeks from embarrassment and illness. She closed the loathsome bag and was surprised when Rand plucked it from her hands and tossed it out the open window. He then offered her his handkerchief, which was the final straw. The unexpected kindness took her by surprise, and more tears rolled down her cheeks.

"Oh, now, don't worry," he clucked, sounding much like Mrs. Peters. "It happens to all of us." He leaned across the aisle, trying to wipe her tears with his hankie, blow her nose like a child, and pat her head like a dog, all at the same time. The students quickly came up with an assortment of paper bags, newspapers, and even one hat.

Kerry looked at their generosity without understanding. "I won't need those now."

"Well, we'll just wait and see. Better to have them and not need them, wouldn't you say?" Rand reasoned, still patting her shoulder, making her feel like a sheep dog.

"I like it when you scratch behind my ears, too," she said, feeling very testy after making such a spectacle of herself.

Rand realized what he was doing and abruptly put his hands in his pockets, turning away with a funny look.

Kerry was ashamed. He had been trying to be helpful, and goodness knows, he really had been. It wasn't his fault that her illness embarrassed her into irritability.

"I'm sorry about being sick and then snippy on top of it," Kerry apologized.

"Twenty minutes," Rand replied.

"Excuse me?" Kerry asked.

"I suggest you try and relax for the next twenty minutes. That's how long it will take your system to rebel against this bus ride again."

Kerry looked at him with dawning horror and closed her eyes against the inevitable. "You're a doctor. Can't you do something?"

"I should have given you something before we left. But I keep forgetting how delicate and reactive American women are to hard travel."

Kerry wanted to hit him over the head. She would have, if the nausea had not come back. Instead, she stuck her tongue out at him. He didn't notice, but she felt slightly better.

And to make things worse, he was right. He'd had

some experience in this matter of "delicate, reactive American women" and Indian bus travel. Kerry was getting her experience the hard way.

Every twenty minutes or so, she earnestly thanked one more person for his container, while Rand pitched it out the window.

"Sister Kerry, you must let Brother Dennison pray for you," Sister Minnie urged.

Kerry's ear was aching, and she really did want to experience a miracle. One of those instantaneous healings would suit her just fine. "All right, Sister Minnie, you ask him."

Kerry knew that she would not die. She would have to get better to die.

Rand and the students leaned over toward her, putting their hands on her head and shoulders. They began to pray, and Kerry felt tears well up in her eyes and a warmth go through her.

When they were done, Kerry felt the tears still hanging on the edge of her bottom lids and willed them to drain. She felt that if she ever started, she would just go on crying and crying until next week.

God did not take away the motion sickness, but her ear stopped aching.

Kerry held her forehead each time the sickness hit, and Sister Minnie braced her back on the other side.

Kerry muscles strained, and her head swam. The bus trip felt as if it were taking months at sea instead of a few hours.

When they finally stopped, Kerry wondered if she could just be buried at the village.

Rand, so helpful on the trip, slapped her shoulder

briskly as if she was one of the football team. He said, "Now you'll be O.K.!" and left her, anxious to get the clinic lined up. Some doctor, Kerry thought darkly.

Kerry staggered off the bus, and the female Bible school students introduced her to the village women, who were preparing curry to eat before service. The pastor's wife came rushing over and asked, through one of the students, if Kerry was all right.

Kerry realized she was still holding her stomach. "Yes, tell her that I got bus sick."

With the interpretation, all the village women nodded their heads sagely, and one called her teenage son over. He took a large knife and a green coconut to the edge of the clearing. Holding the coconut in one hand, he whacked the top off with his knife. Kerry was terrified that he'd miss and remove his hand at the wrist, but she needn't have worried. His mother took the coconut and brought it to Kerry.

The hollow shell and meat made a cup, filled partly with sweet coconut milk that was more like fruit juice than cow's milk. Kerry was thirsty and dehydrated, making it seem like something straight from heaven. The juice was several degrees cooler than the outside temperature.

She sat quietly on a low rock wall and watched as the women prepared vegetables and rice for their meal. They worked in an open-air kitchen, which had a small pit dug for the fire and some grating over the pit that held the pots.

Into a large, heavy iron pan, one woman poured *ghee*, or clarified butter. When it was hot enough so that a drop of water flicked around and spluttered, she added chopped onions and a handful of salt, stirring until they were soft and golden brown.

Then she stirred in uncooked rice, coating it with the hot oil. She also stirred in fresh green beans, carrots, green pepper, cubed potatoes, fresh green peas, and finally, lots of water.

Another woman came over with a covered aluminum *thali* that contained spices. She threw handfuls in the large pot.

The ladies brought the stew, or rather *pilaf*, to a boil and then pulled the pot back from the fire pit so that it would simmer. A large sheet of metal was put over the top.

Minnie appeared by Kerry's side. "You are watching the preparation of *sabzi ka chaval*. It is almost a feast for these poor people, but they always serve the best that they have."

Kerry nodded, feeling humbled. "What do they all do for jobs?"

"Most of them farm wheat in this area and their own vegetables, too. A few do service jobs, and many women make handicrafts to sell at the market or in Delhi, but mostly they farm. Both men and women work in the fields. Their children help them when they're not in the village school. Attendance is required until the children turn twelve."

Rand set up his clinic in the middle of the village, where the elders met. Many people lined up. Some had tumors on their faces or ears. Mothers patiently carried sick children, and strong men held their farming injuries carefully still as they each waited a turn.

Kerry felt so much better now that she was off the bus, and she watched as Rand checked each person. Sometimes he gave them medicine from a small black valise. Sometimes he told them to come back when he had his surgical team with him.

He extracted a tooth from an old woman whose jaw was swollen to twice its normal size.

Kerry's eyes filled with tears when he shook his head negatively over an old man on a stretcher.

Rand lanced boils, stitched cuts, put drops in eyes, and had one mother spit on the ground. Who knew why?

She wouldn't admit it for the world, but Rand was patient and kind with all of them. Why couldn't he be nicer to her? Why did every word seem to provoke her?

When the village women brought her some food on a large leaf, she couldn't eat it. She did wrap it up in the leaf and stick it in her purse with the intention of getting rid of it later. Kerry hated to waste food, but she absolutely could not eat right then, and she did not wish to offend the kind people.

The men, who were served first, ate separately. This did not seem to faze the ladies, who thoroughly enjoyed their visit with each other.

Kerry asked one of them, "Where can I find a rest room and clean up?"

The woman gestured into the brush. No bathrooms! Kerry decided to wait until everyone was in the church service. That way she could be sure no one was around.

She asked for a bowl of hot water to wash her hands. She wrung out a hankie from her purse, wiped her neck and face, and scrubbed her teeth with it.

Minnie called, "Sister Kerry, will you walk with us?" Kerry nodded, smiling. Sister Minnie and the other female students were walking to one of the villager's homes to see an elderly grandma.

The village was small, with less than five hundred people. It did not have a post office or shop, so the villagers bought and sold at nearby market towns or at the weekly market, located at the spot where bullock-cart roads from several villages met.

"We must go to the lower part of town," one of the students informed Kerry. "This village is grouped according to the caste of the people. There is a small Hindu shrine in the middle of the village."

Kerry had seen it, with the elephant-headed idol of Ganesh, near Rand's clinic. Garlands of leaves and flowers were draped over the three-foot-high statue, which resembled a cheap piggy bank to Kerry.

"There are two wells here, although discrimination against the Harijans is outlawed," Minnie added.

"I don't understand."

Minnie dropped her voice. "Below all the castes are the untouchables, whom Gandhi renamed the Harijans, or children of God. They are still treated poorly, even though untouchability was abolished by the Indian constitution. Most of our converts are from this group."

Kerry knew that the standard of living in Indian villages was very low, but she was still amazed when she saw the mud and straw houses. Their thatched roofs covered one or two rooms in which extended families lived. There were no wooden doors or screened windows.

The ladies entered a house, and Kerry found it had little furniture. The grandmother, smiling and pleased with their visit, sat on her bed, which was a pile of straw covered with a carpet. A few cotton quilts were folded at her feet, which were greatly deformed and twisted from arthritis.

Above her bed, a photo and a postcard were tacked to the wall. The brightly colored postcard was an artist's rendition of Jesus with small children around him, and the photo was of Dr. Dennison, surrounded by students, standing in front of the Bible school.

Sister Minnie made the introductions. "Sister Chandra welcomes you to her son's home. She is very proud of her photo gallery above her bed, because she used to have pictures of her many Hindu gods up there. But now she is proud to be a Christian, and she also knows that praying to pictures does no good. She just likes to look at them for joy, and she prays directly to Jesus."

Kerry nodded and smiled and suddenly dug in her purse for her wallet.

Sister Minnie looked appalled. "You will offend her hospitality if you give her money."

"No, this is a different gift for her." Kerry grinned and found her high school graduation photo and the business card from her dad's church, which had a small picture of the building on it.

"Explain that this is the church I grew up in, and this photo is a few years old, but it is still me," Kerry said to Minnie as she handed the items into the gnarled hands, holding the old fingers gently for a few moments.

Sister Chandra smiled and nodded, obviously pleased to have a reminder of this visit.

The ladies crowded around the bed, laying hands on the woman to pray. They made room for Kerry, and she found herself putting her hand on the woman's shoulder.

It had been a long time since she had prayed for anyone.

"O God," she breathed, "please bless this dear woman, and give her comfort and rest in her crippled body. And forgive me for complaining so often, when I have so much more than she will ever have."

Kerry wiped her eyes when they were all finished.

Filing out of the house, Kerry realized that Sister Chandra, in her poverty, was far more content with her life than she was in her affluence.

"Ladies!" Rand called from across the clearing, "we are ready to start service!"

Kerry decided that this would be a great time to sneak away. Twilight made it easy to slip off from the group, and she walked back to the makeshift kitchen. She couldn't see or hear anyone around, so she moved into the trees and bushes and looked for a sheltered spot.

Kerry knew which direction she had come from and set off at a brisk walk. But somehow, in the growing darkness, it seemed different. She couldn't hear the church group, and she began to feel a little panicky.

She walked back but could not find her original destination. Where was she?

That was when she heard the low growl. It wasn't close. It didn't seem very close. Surely it couldn't be close, please, please, please! But she could hear something. It was probably a monkey or a bird.

Kerry thought about shouting. That ought to bring everyone running. Of course, it might attract unfriendly visitors, too. Kerry wished she could find a landmark.

Just as she turned to go yet another way, she heard the crackle immediately behind her. Her first instinct, which she obeyed with all speed, was to crouch down low and stop breathing.

All was quiet.

Kerry let her breath out in a silent stream and wondered if animals could really smell fear. She had nothing to fight off a predator. She could feel hot breath on her neck.

What was the rule with bears? Do you lie down and pretend to be dead, or do you roll on your back to show a submissive posture? Or was she thinking of wolves? Kerry decided her best bet was to cover her head and stomach by rolling into a ball and being still.

She heard the movement by her right shoulder seconds before she felt it.

# EIGHT

**SOMETHING TOUCHED** Kerry's shoulder. She whirled, ready to strike out, but jumped back when she saw a Naga, covered in ash, standing before her. She was suddenly glad of the twilight and kept her gaze on his face, looking at the dark brown eyes that watched her curiously. She realized, with a start, that he was the same Naga from the school courtyard.

Then he turned and motioned once, walking off into the darkness. Kerry wasn't sure if following was foolish or not, but she was running out of options. She ran, trying to keep up with his long strides.

How did he get here? He didn't come on the bus, and he had been sick in one of the schoolrooms just that afternoon. Could this really be the same one?

Yes, I think it is, Kerry argued with herself, even though I only saw him for a moment. His eyes are too distinctive to mistake.

Kerry started to see light in the distance from the oil lamps that the church members used when darkness fell. The Naga stopped at the edge of the clearing, where no one in the village could see him, and waited while

Kerry caught up.

"Thank you," she said. "I don't know if you understand, but you were just what I needed."

She reached into her purse, got out the leaf-wrapped meal, and passed it to him. He silently took it, turned around, and disappeared into the dark. Kerry heard another growl from the darkness, but much closer this time.

"O Jesus, keep him safe," she whispered.

The service was getting started, and no one seemed to have noticed that she was just now arriving. Kerry relaxed as she found a seat among the others, perching on a wooden stump.

The missionaries had come here about a year ago. Then Rand began visiting with his medical team. Now, one of the former Bible school students was the pastor of this small group of worshipers. It was considered a big event when the Bible school students came for a service. The pastor's wife had explained all of this to Kerry during the meal preparation, using one of the students as an interpreter.

Kerry watched as some of the villagers who had not come for the church service took a camel off the round grinding stone in the middle of the village square. The camel wore a blindfold and walked slowly around in a circle all day.

Kerry could well identify with that camel. She felt as though she blindly walked through life, letting others lead her. First, her family as she grew up, which was to be expected up to a point, and now her job and friends. Would she ever be in control of her future?

Women passed by, balancing large, earthen water jars

on their heads. Kerry noted that a small jar nestled in the neck of the large jar and wondered how they got them up there.

The worship began, and the people stood, raising hands to heaven, smiling, and singing. Kerry did not know the song, for it had an unusual sound with fewer notes in the scale, but she raised her hands anyway.

"I love You, Lord," she began, speaking a quiet prayer. "I really do, You know," she went on. "I know it hasn't seemed like it lately, but I remember how it used to be. I . . . I miss . . . feeling Your love. I miss . . . talking to You, Lord."

Kerry talked to God as she talked with any of her friends, with directness and truth. She went on, "I've tried to be independent, Lord, but I'm not very happy. I don't want to go back to being a child, simply doing what my parents expect, and I don't want to continue on this way either. Do You have any place for me, Lord? Can You forgive me and love me?"

When God answered Kerry's simple prayer, He used the language of *agape* love, warming her heart and reassuring her soul of His unfailing love.

Kerry was unaware that her face was wet and shining with repentance and peace. She looked radiantly beautiful, her arms lifted and her words praising God again and again.

The people worshiped and prayed for almost an hour. Finally the pastor bid them sit down for the rest of the service. Kerry hated to stop, she was so starved for God's refreshing love.

Minnie sat next to her to interpret the testimonies of the people. Rand sat down on the other side. Minnie started, "This man says that they have been living in fear because the local authorities have threatened to arrest them for holding Christian services. He says that he feels freedom from that fear now that we are here."

A young woman stood to speak, weeping as she talked. "She is telling us how a leopard, wounded by poachers, has been preying on the village children this past month. She says that she found one of the ravaged bodies on her way to the river last week. She has had great fear for her own children and has been having horrible nightmares about it. She asks us to pray for her."

Rand spoke quietly, adding, "The land is so crowded that the animals have no room to hunt, and so they often turn upon the people. India is one third the size of the United States, but she has three times as many people."

An elderly man stood and began to testify. Rand interpreted this time: "He says that he and his wife had no food to eat before the monsoon rains came last year. This village is poor, and he cannot work in the fields anymore. He and his wife were starving. But when they were ready to die, they knelt and prayed to the one true God, Jesus, to see if there was any power there. The next day, his daughter came to visit him from the city, for the first time in many years, bringing enough food for a month. He thanks God, the one true God, because they have never been hungry since that day. They threw their Hindu gods in the river and stopped paying the local guru."

Kerry glanced over. Rand seemed very absorbed in his thoughts.

"Rand, do you really believe God answered their

prayers, or was it just a coincidence that their daughter came?"

He turned and smiled at her. "I guess the answer depends on whether you choose to trust God or coincidence to answer your needs. Have you ever really needed anything, Kerry? These people depend upon God for survival, not comfort."

Kerry looked away. He hadn't answered her question at all. Or had he?

All the students and church members gathered around to pray for the sick. Rand joined them with complete ease, praying for some of the same ones he had just treated in his clinic.

Then it was time for the sermon. A small man with a gentle smile, whom they addressed as Lera, began to speak.

"He is a great evangelist who has won thousands of people to Christ," Minnie whispered. "He grew up in a village like this one."

His words were confident and strong, even though Kerry could not understand the language he spoke.

A tall man with a turbaned head came walking over to the group as they held their service in the open air, having no church building. He began to shout. Kerry couldn't understand a word, but it was apparent that he was challenging the missionaries. She wondered if he could arrest them, or have them arrested, for holding the service.

"Sister Kerry," Minnie sounded close to tears, "he is saying that the village elders have voted against having a Christian church or hospital here. But Rand and Lera are asking him to let the villagers decide by coming out to the clinic and church service next week. He is not happy but says he will tell the elders."

The man walked off, leaving the congregation in disquiet. Lera began to lead the people in prayer, while the students knelt to intercede for the villagers.

Kerry felt the heaviness of the man's threat. When had she ever been threatened for coming to church? Never. She joined the others on their knees and began to pray for others this time.

When the group finished, it was time to catch the bus. The pastor's wife passed her a cup of tea before the journey home, motioning for Kerry to drink all of it. Kerry hoped it was boiled. Even if it was not, it tasted marvelous, and she finished it all. She dreaded the ride back and wondered how she would endure it.

The tired group climbed back on the bus after it pulled up next to the village. This time, Rand motioned Kerry into a seat and sat beside her. "Just in case," he muttered.

Most of the students quickly nodded off to sleep on the darkened bus. Kerry felt drowsy, too.

"Did you drink your herbal?" Rand asked.

"My what?"

"I told the pastor's wife that you needed something to make your journey home easier. She was going to brew you an herbal."

"I drank a home remedy? I might die!"

Rand smiled. "I thought you were going to do that on the way here."

"Well, maybe. I hope it won't make me sick again." This sentence ended in a huge yawn as Kerry's herbal began its effective work.

"Rand, why do the women have to eat apart, and later?"

He sighed. "Some traditions are centuries old. I've only been coming to this village within the past year. Give me some time," he teased her.

The country roads were inky black. Only the lights of the bus cut through the absolute darkness. Rand felt the letdown after his rushed clinic and the confrontational service. The sudden absence of hustle and bustle increased his fatigue.

This trip back to the school was far more relaxed for Rand than the earlier one because his seat companion was not ill anymore. The fact that she was cute didn't hurt the situation either.

Kerry decided that if she could just keep her mind on something other than getting ill, she could tough out this trip back into the city. So she pumped Rand for information.

"Rand, would you please explain about castes to me? I understand that you can lose caste, but I thought you were born into a caste."

That was all Rand needed. He was like a tour tape. If you pushed the right button, information came pouring out without interruption.

"Ah, the caste system. In existence since Aryans entered India, around 1500 B.C. The four original castes were ranked in terms of ritual purity and occupation, with the Brahmins (priests) at the top, followed by the warrior and ruler Kshatriyas. The teachers and merchants were Vaishyas, and the native Indians, or Dravidians, were called Sudras. Sudras were not allowed to marry Aryans."

"Didn't the Nazis call themselves the Aryan nation?"

"Yes, but Aryans came over the Caucasus mountain region into the Indus Valley civilization thousands of years before the Nazis were around.

"Anyway," he went on, "in India you are born into a caste, and no matter how much education or money you earn, you have no upward mobility in the caste system."

Kerry vaguely remembered studying the rigidity of the system in school.

"Caste regulates whom you marry, what vocation you choose, and what you may eat. A Brahmin, for example, may not take water or food cooked or served by a member of a lower caste. Which explains why so many Brahmins become chefs."

"Our driver from the airport was a Brahmin, right?" Kerry quickly put together.

"Yes, and his brother is a chef," he nodded.

"When a Hindu 'breaks caste,' it means that he sins against the requirements of his caste and will have to work his way back with time, offerings, and penance until he is accepted in the sight of his gods again. So no one wants to break caste."

"I noticed the two wells at the village," Kerry interrupted. "One was for Hindus and the other for Untouchables. That must be because they do not wish to break caste."

"That is correct. I have a special interest in the group that most consider outside the caste system, because my missionary friends do most of their work with them. For them, access to a loving God is a new and wonderful concept."

"You mean they couldn't even be Hindus because of their low caste?" Kerry questioned.

"Only through many cycles of reincarnation, hopefully moving up each time, would they ever reach *nirvana*, or complete joy and happiness. Not a friendly system for the low born."

"Well, that helps me understand a little better. Tyler said that you are planning a charity hospital for them at the school."

Rand frowned. "Trust Tyler to get his facts wrong."

"You're not starting a hospital?"

"Oh, I'm trying to start a permanent clinic, but not the way Tyler thinks I am. I'm not looking for a big medical building with my name on it."

Kerry shook her head. "Rand, why would Tyler think that?"

"Tyler doesn't understand anyone who uses his money or influence for a cause that doesn't turn a healthy profit."

"I think you're being unfair to him!"

"I'm sure you do, but that doesn't change things. A rural hospital, or health center, would include a dispensary with four to six hospital beds, a doctor, several nurses, and midwives. We are talking about a small medical clinic. Most patients won't be able to pay, and the whole thing would have to be supported by donations from the wealthy or possibly a paying clinic in the city. Not a sound business plan for those looking for a fast way to make a buck," Rand said quickly.

"I've found Tyler to be very generous to the girls and me."

Rand smirked and said, "I'm sure you have."

"Well, at least he's been kind enough to let us stay in his home," Kerry added, determined not to speak poorly of her host.

"Listen, I'm sorry," Rand sighed. "I'm just tired and grumpy. But I'm especially glad that you're not sick this half of the journey, because I enjoy these trips to the villages. They are very much like trips I took with my father as a young boy."

Kerry sat back and relaxed. She felt very peaceful.

Rand's voice was soothing, and her eyes were beginning to feel heavy.

He continued, "Dad and I would go out to villages, and as close as ten miles out of the city we could see herds of blackbuck antelope frisking through fields of wheat and mustard."

Kerry felt tranquilized, seeing the pictures that he painted with words.

"On our way back home, we would often stop to watch a water hole as we ate the dinner my mother would pack. At twilight, we would watch each type of animal approach the water. Each one comes to drink differently. Sambar deer stay next to the tree line, anxious and twitching. Barking deer, looking like red lap dogs, come bouncing through the tall grass."

Kerry yawned and sank lower on the bus seat.

"I've seen boars run straight to the water, each trying to be first. However, if a young bull elephant goes down into the hole, he'll drink, spray himself and then crash off, trumpeting, ears flapping. It's quite a show, as long as he's not coming toward you."

He looked over at Kerry, who had only one eye open. She nodded drowsily.

"Am I boring you?" he asked gently.

"Oh, no, I think it's fascinating. I just feel very tired. I may close my eyes and listen, so go on."

He smiled, wondering how much sedative the pastor's wife had stirred into that tea. He'd given her enough of the powder for a big man, not knowing how much of the herbal tea Kerry would be able to drink.

Rand deliberately spoke in a soothing monotone. "There are also the bull gaurs, the largest cattle in the world. They stand six feet at the shoulder and look like a water buffalo on steroids, with their proportionately little heads and little feet. The mynah birds like to land on their backs."

"We lived on the southern edge of New Delhi, and jackals would slip into the garden almost every evening. Now the wildlife of India is far reduced, in competition with all the people."

Kerry roused herself enough to ask, "Did your mother like India?"

"I think she was in love with my father and would have been happy in Antarctica, if that was where he chose to live. You know, ancient literature says that the Indian wife is 'half the man, his truest friend, a perpetual spring of virtue, pleasure, and wealth.' I think it must be a great comfort to have a relationship like that."

Kerry was already fast asleep, as much from exhaustion as from soothing natural herbs and the dose of medicine. Her head lolled to the side and finally flopped on Rand's shoulder. He was a bit startled and reached to wake her, or move her over, when she began to snore.

It was a very soft snore and somehow endearing, because he knew she would hate to be caught so vulnerable. Instead, he shifted his shoulder down to a more agreeable height, propped his knees up on the back of the seat in front of him and enjoyed the coziness.

# NINE

**KERRY AWOKE** to find Mrs. Peters putting a steaming cup of tea next to her bed.

"How on earth did I get here? The last I remember, I was starting that long bus ride back home."

Mrs. Peters smiled at her use of "home." Perhaps she had been concentrating too long on getting Gwen married when she should have been working on Mr. Greyson. After all, he was a widower, and with a young wife there would soon be children to look after, Mrs. Peter's favorite occupation. It was too bad that Kathryn and Danielle weren't really Miss Carlyle's. What a perfect package that would be!

"Why, you were asleep on your feet when Minnie led you in last night. And no wonder! She told us how ill you had been on the first half of the trip. Gwen looked you over to make sure you were really alive, and I helped get you out of your clothes. Gwen wants to get the formula for that herbal from the village women. She said that it was marvelous. You were out like a light."

Kerry blushed bright pink to think that Rand might have seen her drooling in her sleep last night on the bus!

Did she sleep with her mouth hanging open? She cringed at the thought.

She reached for the tea and saw her Bible on the night stand. She pulled it into her lap and opened it to the Book of Acts, reading the first three chapters as she sipped from her cup.

When she was done, she thought back to the previous evening's service and her own conversation with God. Putting the teacup back on the tray and climbing out of bed, she knelt down.

"Dear Jesus, thank You for blotting out my sins and bringing a time of refreshing to my heart. But I sadly lack power in You. I need help when I start to think and act according to my own wisdom instead of Yours. Will You help me? I know I need to be filled with Your power and wisdom instead of my own."

"Miss Carlyle?" came a call up the stairs.

"Yes?" she called back, interrupted in her prayer.

"I have breakfast ready, if you'll come down now," Mrs. Peters called.

"Coming!" Kerry yelled and then muttered, "They didn't have Mrs. Peters on the Day of Pentecost."

Kerry quickly dressed in the icy blue, wrinkle-free dress, tying a matching scarf around her long ponytail. She found Kathryn and Danielle in the kitchen eating big, warm cinnamon rolls that Mrs. Peters had just taken from the oven.

"Oh, those smell wonderful! I missed dinner yesterday, and I think I could eat an elephant!"

That sent the kids into giggles.

"And what did you do last night while I was away?"

"We played jacks and marbles with Mr. Greyson and

Gwen. Mr. Greyson still has all his marbles from when he was a little boy," Danielle volunteered.

Kerry sincerely wondered if she was losing hers . . . marbles that is. It had not occurred to her that Tyler would spend the evening watching the children with Gwen.

"We're helping roof today," Danielle added.

"Who is roofing what?" Kerry asked, mouth half full. A marvelous example for children, she scolded herself.

Mrs. Peters explained. "Rand said that church members from many villages are coming today to put a new roof on the men's dorm wing of the school. They walk in, so by mid-morning it should get very busy and exciting." She frowned. "There's to be a big meal around four, when they're finished. But I thought I would send these rolls over for a work break. Goodness knows, they'll need them, if that school cook is making the afternoon meal!"

Kerry wondered just how bad the meals were over at the school. She observed the many pans of cinnamon rolls that Mrs. Peters had prepared, taking up every available work surface in the kitchen.

"Did you two talk with Rand in his office yesterday?" Kerry asked the small, sticky faces at the table.

They nodded solemnly.

"Yes . . . and . . . ?"

Danielle, always the spokesperson, said, "We are on garbage crew today at the school because we ran off and didn't tell anyone where we were."

"And what exactly is the garbage crew?" Mrs. Peters asked, terrified that they might try and pick up after the roofers, under the eaves, where they could get hurt.

Danielle swallowed, licking her lips while explaining.

"When the big meal is served tonight, we have to pass the garbage containers around and pick up anything that people forget."

Kerry and Mrs. Peters sighed in unison, their relief great.

The girls gave Mrs. Peters some hugs and thank-yous for their breakfast while Kerry thought how well mannered they were. Their mother must have been very nice.

"Also, Minnie gave us a box of charity clothes to dress up in," Danielle called over her shoulder as they slipped out into the garden.

"Do you ever hear Kathryn speak in sentences?" Mrs. Peters asked when they'd gone.

Kerry paused. "Come to think of it, no. She answers in monosyllables. She points and says please, if she wants something. I've occasionally seen her whisper to Danielle, but I don't know if that's just a game or real words. Why?"

Mrs. Peters was drying a glass, and Kerry thought it might get worn down to a nub, such vigor and concentration were being expended on it. "Because my friend down the street, who cooks for another family, has a four-year-old grandson who talks without ceasing. He uses full sentences and grown-up words, although incorrectly. I just wondered if there was a problem, perhaps connected to her parent's death."

Kerry saw the girls pass by the window, carrying the large box of charity clothes. "I know that kids often revert back to earlier behavior when they're experiencing some stress," she replied to Mrs. Peter's astute observation. "So it might be connected. Or maybe it's easier to let Danielle say whatever needs to be said."

They both smiled at that, because Danielle never

lacked words to express herself.

The phone rang in the library, and Mrs. Peters went to answer it while Kerry finished her roll.

"That was the police department," Mrs. Peters announced. "They are sending an officer over to take a statement from you about the Gundersons' burglary."

"You know, Mrs. Peters, it's a miracle that I grabbed the children's passports from the office before we left. They were in a file marked "Travel" that Rand noticed and called to my attention when Koshou was packing overnight bags."

"Oh, yes," Mrs. Peters agreed. "It would be difficult to get them replaced quickly, and no one leaves India without a passport."

"Mrs. Peters! You're right! I've just remembered something. The Gundersons' passports were all in there! I only grabbed the children's, so that must mean their parents did not plan on leaving!"

Mrs. Peters stood quietly. Kerry looked at her expectantly. "It also means that they may not be alive," Mrs. Peters said unhappily.

The front doorbell rang. It was a polite police officer who spoke English very slowly.

Kerry was almost an hour with him before he was satisfied with her statement. However, he offered no hope of recovery for the Gundersons' possessions.

When they were finished, Kerry walked over to the school to watch the roofers and found a crowd. The spectators were yelling and throwing mud, rotten vegetables, and even rocks at the men as they tried to attach the new roof tiles.

Minnie rushed out of the building and pulled Kerry

inside. "The neighborhood Hindu leader has organized some of his followers to make things difficult today."

Kerry felt so angry! She wanted to go out in front of the school and yell at them all. But she knew that yelling was not going to work. How could she break up that crowd?

"Sister Minnie, I need to do something," she explained inadequately as she ran out the back door of the school. She made record time between the buildings and ran into the Greysons' at break-neck speed, colliding with Mrs. Peters.

"Do you have any firecrackers?" she gasped.

Mrs. Peters knew where a box of fireworks remained, left over from January's Republic Day Celebration in New Delhi.

Kerry explained the plan and soon had Mrs. Peters as an enthusiastic helper. Together they slipped over to the school, running up the stairs to the women's dorm while the female students huddled in the main level offices.

Once Kerry and Mrs. Peters figured out which room and window were most advantageous to their plan, they opened the box of fireworks. Carefully, they lit and threw lighted firecrackers from the second-story windows toward the demonstrators and rock throwers.

Boom! Boom! Boom!

Yelps and running feet were heard, but no more vicious threats. Best of all, no more pelting rocks harassed the workers.

Mrs. Peters and Kerry grinned at each other, pleased with themselves. "You know," Mrs. Peters said, "I wish you never had to leave but lived with us permanently. Mr. Greyson adores the children."

Kerry suddenly sobered. What a thought. She was

going to leave in a couple of days and take those sweet kids back to the States where they would all have to face the future.

That future did not include the children's parents. It did include a new way of life, in someone's home, whom they didn't know. And what were the odds of finding another Mrs. Peters at the end of the line waiting for them?

Or waiting for me, Kerry thought irrelevantly, not that she cared.

"You two?" a voice behind them asked.

Rand had come down from the roof to see who was doing the crowd control. He'd been a little apprehensive that the little girls were somehow involved, however unlikely it may have seemed. But Mrs. Peters? That Carlyle woman was a bad influence, he thought, exasperated beyond all belief.

"Did you know," he sternly began, "that Mohandas Gandhi was buried in Raj Ghat, not far from here? It is unfortunate that a Hindu leaves a better testimony and example of nonviolence than those who follow Jesus." Unfortunately, he went on. "Thank you for trying to help, but I'm going to have a hard time convincing these people that we've come to help them if we give them burns from exploding firecrackers. And I'm not very good at plastic surgery, if one of those fireworks decides to go off in your hands, near your faces!" He wasn't quite yelling.

Fireworks were so dangerous, he shivered at the thought of Kerry holding one in her hand. He didn't want to think about the damage it would cause. "Have you ever seen anyone with eyes, ears, or fingers missing from explosive burns? You can thank God that you didn't hurt anyone," he ended and left the room.

Kerry felt sick. Maybe it was the aftermath of being ill last night, but probably not, she thought. She felt faint when she thought of the damage she could have caused. Mrs. Peters looked ashen and shocked.

The two of them walked home slowly, embarrassed after they had been so exhilarated moments before. Kerry went to her room for a nap, and Mrs. Peters decided to go over and help that incompetent cook get a meal ready for the hungry workers.

They say that despite his diminutive size, Napoleon could command people with such skill that they would do anything for him. The same could be said for Mrs. Peters, who single-handedly conquered the school kitchen.

Consumed with guilt, Mrs. Peters found reserves she didn't know she had, in an effort to correct her wrongs. She marched over, found the frustrated cook, and offered her services. He agreed, not seeing the gathering force behind such a small woman. Mrs. Peters reorganized the school kitchen, pulled in three students to help, and began to cook.

The main dish was a savory chicken and vegetable stew over rice. It was delicious and smelled heavenly.

Mrs. Peters discovered one source of the cook's difficulties. He was cooking all vegetables to a burned mush as the base of most of the curries and then using too many spices to cover the burn. She straightened that out and also taught him how to make a quick fruit cobbler for large groups.

Mrs. Peters overcame the language barrier that day as she took a large mixing bowl and measured, with a quart container, four quarts of flour, four quarts of sugar, a handful of salt, a handful of baking powder, four pounds of melted butter, eight eggs, and one quart of chopped cashews. She had the cook stir it until it was mixed and then started chopping mango and papaya flesh into the batter.

As a girl in England, she had used apples to make it for all her brothers and sisters, but apples were hard to get in India. She liked the tropical fruit, though. Sometimes she added coconut. Finally she started filling the long cake pans with batter and baking them until they were golden brown.

When the cook tasted a piece, he grinned and shook her hand. Apparently desserts had eluded him until now. All in all, it was going to be a wonderful meal.

In the Greysons' house, Kerry was alone. She dragged herself up to the guest room, kneeling by her bed. She wept and wept, feeling so horribly ashamed of her violence. She could hardly believe how far from Jesus' example she had strayed. When had she stopped recognizing the difference between her own solutions and His?

Finally after an overdue cleansing of the heart, Kerry began to receive the comfort of the Holy Ghost. Her stomach relaxed from the tense knotting of guilt. Her mind cleared, and her headache disappeared. She began to praise and worship God, the One who loves and forgives broken spirits.

Kerry eventually joined the kitchen staff, looking fresh and calm, the stress lines erased from around her eyes. She prepared the big pans of rice herself, having picked up a few skills from watching at the village. She also helped to serve the workers as they came off the roof. Rand must still be up there, she guessed.

Finally, the serving crew, along with Kerry, sat down and ate. She dutifully added her garbage to the large containers that Kathryn and Danielle were carrying around.

For a punishment, they were having a pretty good time, she thought with great humor and looked for Rand to tell him so. She couldn't find him anywhere. She knew he'd been working with the men. They were all here, enjoying their meal, but where was Rand?

Rand was upstairs, standing in his office, looking at another threatening letter. Who was putting them on his desk? This one read, "We will destroy you and those you love."

Rand walked over to his window, which overlooked the courtyard where everyone was eating. Without a second thought, he checked for Kerry's long ponytail and then two small, blond heads. He found Mrs. Peters in the group and Gwen, bandaging one worker's hand. Minnie was working in the serving line, and he couldn't immediately see anyone missing except for Tyler, who was at the factory.

Rand wandered back to his desk and put his head down on his crossed arms, just to close his eyes for a second before he went down to eat. He was so tired. And why did anyone think he had loved ones here? All his family were back in the States. He didn't have anyone here that he loved.

That is where Kerry found him an hour later. She was hoping to speak to him about the passports. There were so many confusing twists in the disappearance of the Gundersons that she wanted to talk to someone about it!

He must be worn out, she thought, looking at the sunburned back of his neck. He should have worn a hat today. Gently, she shook his shoulder.

"Wake up, Cinderella, you're missing the ball."

Rand struggled back up from the bottom of an ocean of tiredness, trying to focus his eyes. He yawned hugely and stretched.

"You've missed your dinner, and now the workers are getting ready to leave," Kerry informed him.

"Oh, no! I must thank them!" He leaped to his feet with renewed energy and ran out of the office.

Kerry was left staring at his empty chair. She saw the telltale pasted letters of the latest note and turned it around to read it better.

The threat was violent.

They must mean the children! They had been helping with the cleanup, but Kerry hadn't seen them in a while. She ran down to find them.

This time she started at the Greysons' house, checking the garden, kitchen, and nursery. No one seemed to be home.

Then she noticed that Mrs. Peters was lying down on the couch, asleep after coping with the huge meal. Kerry didn't awaken her.

She ran back to the old stables, wondering if the girls were playing with the elephant. It was still and quiet in the stables, with no sign of the elephant's keeper. Tiptoe swung her head around to look at Kerry when she opened the side door. No children were there.

She ran back to the school, bounding up the stairs to the women's dorm. The ladies were chattering, changing, and doing their studies, but none had seen Danielle or Kathryn.

Maybe they were in the back of the school, where

garbage was dumped. Kerry flew down the steps, out the back door, and past the school vegetable garden. There was the dump, but there were no children.

She raced back into the school to find Rand and located him in the front courtyard.

"I thank you so much. Your work is appreciated," Rand was saying to the last group of village men on their way out of the gates. He turned around to find a wild-eyed Kerry.

"I cannot find them! They've taken them!" she said, hysterically.

"What? Who?"

"Danielle and Kathryn! The threat on your desk! Or maybe their parents!" she rambled. Her voice was rising, and she couldn't put her thoughts or sentences together properly.

Rand took her by the shoulders and lifted her up until she was inches from his face. "What are you saying?" he gritted out.

"I can't find the children anywhere!"

# TEN

"**FOLLOW ME!**" Rand demanded and didn't wait to see if she came. Kerry ran to keep up with his long, fast strides. He crossed over to the Greysons' property and then back toward the stables.

"I've already checked there!" she called.

"It doesn't matter," he answered.

"What do you mean, it doesn't matter?"

He pushed open the side door and stepped in. Kerry almost ran into the back of him as he stopped and called out. "Coooeee, coooeee!"

Tiptoe turned to see who was visiting and raised her trunk in greeting.

"See, I told you I had already looked," she wailed, terrified that they'd wasted good time.

A faint answer, "Cooooeee," came from the back of the barn.

"They're O.K.," he said with relief.

"They are?"

Walking toward the elephant, Rand held Kerry's hand as he led her behind Tiptoe toward an old *hoodah* in the corner. The curtained elephant saddle, which dignitaries used many years ago to travel on an elephant's back, looked like a little playhouse. It was covered with dust, but one of the curtains twitched, and there sat Danielle and Kathryn having a picnic with some of Mrs. Peters cinnamon rolls piled on a napkin.

They crawled out and Rand sat down on a pile of straw, crossing his legs as they both crawled in his lap and put their arms around him. "What happened?" he asked kindly.

"What happened?" Kerry repeated. "And how did you know where to find them?" she added, sitting cross-legged next to him and pulling Kathryn into her lap for a reassuring hug.

Danielle brightened, anxious to relay the adventure. "We were taking the garbage out to the dump in back of the school when a man we didn't know came out from behind some bushes. He smiled at us, but he looked like a pirate. So we threw the garbage at his feet and ran into the garden, keeping under the hedges. He started to chase us, but we doubled back and slipped over here to hide behind Tiptoe, just like you told us."

Rand smiled his approval and nodded his head.

"You knew this might happen?" Kerry squeaked.

"I knew that anyone watching the school would quickly figure out that I was most vulnerable through the children."

"Rand told us that if anyone was looking at us or following us, so that we felt uncomfortable, we should lose them in the garden and meet him back here. He would give us the signal that it was him; otherwise we needed to keep perfectly still in that little playhouse."

Kerry was watching Rand closely. How could she have ever managed without him thinking ahead like this?

"Thank you for having the forethought to plan this," she said solemnly, catching his attention. "I could never repay you for protecting them so well."

"Why, Sister Kerry, such gratitude!" He winked at her. "I've already thought of something . . . to repay me that is."

"What?" she asked, feeling wary.

He leaned over toward her. "Can you make me something to eat, so that I don't have to ask the cook?"

Kerry laughed. He might be normal after all. "Of course! I shall be honored," Kerry intoned, standing and bowing from the waist like a servant.

Together the four of them walked back to the Greysons' to be met by Mrs. Peters and Bubbles in the garden.

"I was just looking for you girls!" Mrs. Peters smiled. "You were such excellent helpers today, and I am far too tired to cook another meal, so I thought we would walk down to Mrs. Smith's kitchen and join her. She's been wanting to meet you. When she found out that I'd helped with the big dinner, she insisted that we come. She's making mango ice cream for dessert!"

The girls cheered.

"Is that all right, Miss Carlyle? Gwen and Mr. Greyson are out this evening, and Mrs. Smith cooks for the Fortrains, just three houses down. You could join us. I don't wish to leave you alone, with nothing to eat or do."

Kerry thanked and reassured her that it was going to be a delight to have some quiet time. She was fully capable of a snack for herself and Rand, if Mrs. Peters didn't mind them using her kitchen and pantry.

Mrs. Peters, with a child on each side, walked out of the garden while Rand held the door for Kerry to proceed into the kitchen. "I'm rather filthy," he said, looking at his shirt. "If you don't mind, I'll clean up while you fix something and be right back." Rand was suddenly self-conscious in the confines of the kitchen.

Kerry watched as he left, and as soon as the door closed behind him, ran upstairs to check her own appearance. In the bathroom mirror, she saw a sweaty, dirty face with straw stuck in her hair. She saw the reflection of the dirty blue dress with no wrinkles. How ridiculous! Quickly, Kerry stripped and stepped into the old-fashioned shower. She pulled the chain, and the container, perched up on a shelf, trickled water onto her head. She lathered up and then pulled the chain harder and longer to rinse off. At least she felt cleaner!

She balked at putting on yet another wrinkle-free dress. She was getting tired of looking like some dolly fresh out of its wrappings. Then she noticed, through the door adjoining the nursery, the box of charity play clothes for the girls.

She rifled through them and came up with another long sari, the material a subdued yellow, soft to the touch, with pink edging.

This time Kerry knew just what to wear under it. She carried it back to her room and dug into her bag. Yes, here it was: a loose silk blouse, cut in a wide boat neck with bell-shaped, elbow-length sleeves. It was very modest, but cool and flattering and just perfect for under the sari.

Now if she could just remember how to wrap it. Kerry twisted herself in front of the mirror. She wrapped and unwrapped it a few times until she anchored the whole thing with a few hidden safety pins.

Then she took her hair that was drying rapidly and brushed it till it curled around her face and fell in a waterfall to her waist. She had no idea why she was acting so silly. It wasn't as if she cared what Rand thought of her. Maybe she just wanted to erase the horrible impression she'd left on the bus and with the fireworks. She certainly didn't want Rand to remember her that way!

And so, when Rand showed up, fifteen minutes later, he opened the door to find the most exotically beautiful creature he'd ever seen. It was such an interesting mixture of Eastern dress on a Western figure, with an angelic face and auburn and gold tresses. He wasn't sure this was such a good idea after all. On the other hand, he wasn't about to leave.

"Er . . . you look great. I mean," he caught himself, "you look like you've made something great," Rand choked.

Kerry smiled. She could see that her appearance had taken him back a bit. Well, good. She was glad she'd taken the time.

Rand sat in one of the chairs pulled up to the large kitchen table and watched while Kerry stirred eggs in a bowl, dumping them into a hot skillet with onions, cheese, and mushrooms. His mouth watered.

"You must be very tired, but the roof looks good. You're probably happy to have it all finished," Kerry said conversationally as she pulled toast from the oven and buttered it, adding it to the plate of eggs. She'd also found some cold boiled potatoes to slice and fry. They were crisp and ready. She placed the huge platter in front of Rand, along with a glass of orange juice, freshly squeezed that morning.

"I think I've died and gone to heaven!" he said rapturously.

"I think you're exhausted out of your mind," she answered dryly.

He prayed quickly and wondered if his eyes would roll back in his head from pleasure as he scooped in the first mouthful. After that, the careful construction of eggs and potatoes perched on pieces of toast kept Rand too busy to talk. Kerry kept refilling his glass and watching him eat enormous amounts of food.

Finally, sitting back from the table, eating Mrs. Peters homemade oatmeal cookies and a glass of milk, Rand looked up to find Kerry doing the dishes. She was never more beautiful to him. The steam from the water added a moist film to her skin, and her hair kinked up around her face.

He took his empty glass over to the sink and picked up a dry towel. His own mother had taught him the basics a long time ago. He couldn't remember the last time he'd dried any dishes, but it seemed very appealing this evening.

"Don't do that!" Kerry cried. "You've been working all day. Go home and get some sleep. This is nothing to clean up."

"I would enjoy the company," he said simply, and they finished in companionable silence.

Untying the towel around her waist, which was somewhat damp, Kerry spotted a spider on the floor. In a funny mood, she snapped him with her towel, sending him to spider heaven in a hurry.

"I am impressed. So many, many talents. I think I would like to display my admiration," Rand murmured as he stepped closer and put his hands on her shoulders.

Kerry stood very still, breathless, as she felt his lips touch the right side of her face on her cheekbone.

"Hullo! Anyone home?" they heard from the front hallway.

Kerry felt the blush rise as Rand stepped abruptly away from her. He walked out the garden door before she could say a word.

"Oh, there you are. Don't you look terribly domestic!" Tyler exclaimed as he walked into the kitchen.

"Making yourself a snack? I could do with one myself, would you mind?" he added.

Kerry nodded dumbly and felt as if she were having déjà vu. "Would eggs be all right?" she asked weakly.

"Yes, but I like them done in just a certain way, so I'll come and help," Tyler said, shrugging off his perfectly tailored jacket and turning up the snowy white sleeves. He even took off his silk tie, folding it neatly on top of the jacket.

Kerry couldn't help but notice that he looked like a male model in an advertisement. His smile was perfect, his hair was perfect, and he was in trim form. Didn't he ever get messed up?

Tyler was a good cook, and he stayed immaculate. Kerry found herself enjoying the preparation. He was delightful, entertaining her with funny stories, teasing and telling her that she was sweeter than crumpets.

Kerry remembered Rand's look when he entered the kitchen earlier. She hadn't imagined that. It gave her a very warm feeling, and she laughed at Tyler's jokes with more enthusiasm than they deserved.

When she began to clear the plates to wash up, Tyler stopped her.

"Mrs. Peters will do that tomorrow. That's what I pay her for, so you must come and humor an old man. Let's walk out in the garden and see if we can find the jasmine."

Kerry decided to join him and clean up later. The cool night air felt wonderful on her flushed skin. Tyler held out the suit jacket that he had picked up on his way out of the kitchen. He draped it around her shoulders.

Propelling her gently down the path as he held her elbow, Tyler spoke lightly of how he was enjoying the children and Kerry as guests.

"Do you smell it?" he suddenly asked.

"I do smell something. It's wonderful!"

"It's the night-blooming jasmine, the sweetest flower in the world." He turned toward Kerry and put his arm around her. "Except for you, dear; you've brought such happiness into my house."

Kerry froze and then relaxed as he dropped his arm, moved to her side, and continued walking as though he had never stopped. She almost bolted when she thought Tyler was going to kiss her. She didn't know why.

"Well, Kerry, what do you say?"

Again?

"I'm sorry, Tyler, I was distracted. What did you ask me?" Kerry apologized.

Tyler smiled, and his teeth almost gleamed in the darkness. He was very amused.

"Have I distracted you, darling Kerry? Well, bully for me! I was telling you that I've set up a trust for Kathryn and Danielle so that they will never have any financial needs in their little lives. I've also spoken to your people back in Ohio. It turns out that there is only one elderly man on Mrs. Gunderson's side of the family, and he is ill.

The children have no one to turn to, and the courts will probably appoint a guardian. I've asked if they will consider me."

Kerry was amazed!

"You set up a trust for them? Oh, Tyler, you're so generous! And if the judge appointed you guardian, where would they live?"

"Why, here, of course. I have grown to love the little angels. Do you think an old man like me would have a chance? I'd have Mrs. Peters and Gwen to help, you know."

"Oh, Tyler, I don't know what to say."

Kerry just stared at him. It was the answer to many of their problems. And wouldn't it be nice for the girls to have a family that already loved them?

"Tyler, this is so sudden. You've thought of everything."

"Well, actually, I have," he answered and pulled a little box from his pocket, opening it to reveal a huge, round emerald. It looked priceless.

He pulled out her hand and slipped the ring on. It glittered in dark green beauty in the moonlight. The rounded cabochon surface had an elephant engraved on it. The gold setting looked old. Kerry was mesmerized by it. She had never owned a precious stone in all of her life. It's loveliness was breathtaking.

"Kerry, this is just a small thank-you for all that you've done for us. You brought the children here and have increased my happiness ever so much. Will you come and have that special dinner with me at my club tomorrow evening?" Tyler added.

He saw the way her eyes widened over the emerald, and he decided to let that magic work on its own for a while. Indeed, he had to bite his lip to keep from laughing, because she never looked at him. Rather, Kerry nodded in agreement to dinner, never breaking eye contact with the emerald. He'd seen that response before and understood it only too well.

Tyler pulled Kerry's arm around and walked her back to the kitchen like a guide dog, steering her around bushes and trees. Finally, in the light from the doorway, he kissed her lightly on the cheek and wished her sweet dreams. Kerry never even noticed.

When she finally looked up and noticed that Tyler was gone, her eyes landed on the sink, piled high with dirty dishes. She rushed over and took the ring off, putting it on the window sill, over the faucet, right at eye level. She washed and dried, still enjoying the play of light over the surface. It was like drowning in an ocean or becoming part of a magic cave of wonders. Kerry blocked out everything but her pleasure in the ring, overwhelmed by the beauty of the emerald.

She picked up the ring and went to bed, dreaming of green glades, green waterfalls, and green stars, but never Tyler and not even Rand.

Tyler fell asleep easily and had contented dreams of a house full of children, a beautiful wife dressed in the latest fashion, and a big family running out to greet him as he brought in mountains of presents.

Only Rand was having a miserable evening. What had happened to his brain, he wondered? I probably cooked it on the roof today. Why had he kissed Kerry, and in such a ridiculous way, too? Obviously, the lack of practice had its effects. When I should have been complimentary, I talked about the food.

His pacing left him in front of the mirror. He stopped and looked at his reflection. Awful. His hair stood up on end, his face was sunburnt bright red. His glasses were crooked! When had that happened? His shirt was . . . just like the one his grandpa always wore. No wonder she stood stock still. It was probably either that or run screaming from the kitchen.

Rand determined to do something about himself tomorrow. It was scheduled as a day off for the students, but he would take the day off also. He would go in the morning and take care of a few of these deficiencies.

Muscles aching and too tired to sleep comfortably, Rand went into his office to work. The window looked over the back of the house, toward the Greysons' stables, and Rand grinned to think of Danielle and Kathryn in there, safe, because of his plan.

He was just bending to switch on the desk light when he thought he saw a movement in the Greysons' back yard. Immediately he stood back, so that he could see without being seen.

Instead of prowlers, he saw Tyler and Kerry looking cozy by the back door. In fact, Tyler bent over and kissed Kerry on the cheek and then went into the house. Kerry didn't return the kiss, but neither did she seem to be fighting him off. In fact, she seemed oblivious, looking very intently at her hand. Had she burned it? Was Tyler just being concerned? Not likely.

"That handsome snake in the grass is making time with my girl!" Rand couldn't believe he'd thought that, let alone said it. He groaned. He looked like his grandpa, and now he sounded like him too.

He didn't need a girl; he hadn't time for one. Besides,

Kerry wasn't his girl. She probably couldn't stand him.

Rand paced around the room, muttering and angry. Then abruptly he stopped.

He knelt and began to pray. The prayer went on for a long time as he tried to sort out his thoughts and feelings, presenting them to God. When Rand got up, he didn't look so grim.

Still, he made so many mistakes while trying to do business at his desk that night that in the morning he took it all in to Minnie's office, left her a note to untangle it, and took himself to the barber.

# ELEVEN

**THE MORNING SUN** hit the emerald ring, making a green flame. It was truly marvelous, she thought. Almost distracting, in fact. She shook her head, as if to clear it from the fog, and still couldn't remember what she was supposed to be doing today. She knew that there was something. . . .

"Shoes!" came a clear voice from the nursery. Kerry wondered if she was hearing voices.

"Shoes, shoes, shoes!" yelled Kathryn wearing Kerry's slippers and flip-flopping into the room.

"Well, don't you have a fine voice! And I thought you didn't like to talk," Kerry told the rosebud who was beginning to open up.

"New shoes?"

"Yes, that is what we are doing, isn't it, Kathryn? How clever of you to remember." She pulled the child over for a big, noisy kiss on the forehead. She could very well imagine a lovely life for these children in this beautiful house with Mrs. Peters, Tyler, and Gwen.

Laying out the recently laundered, hot pink, "wrinkle-free wonder," Kerry was determined to buy two saris at the market, along with shoes for the kids. Their shoes were fairly scuffed, and Danielle's had burn marks. She also wanted to talk with Mr. Miller today about the Gundersons' burglary, for which the police claimed they had no leads, and about Tyler's soil report.

First, the market.

Just then Bubbles, the monkey, who was supposed to be living in the barn and not in the house, scampered in through Kerry's window.

"Oh, no! Are you visiting again? Those girls feed you too much. I don't have a thing for you. Sorry."

But Bubbles wasn't looking for handouts. She had a piece of paper in her little fingers. It looked like a photo.

Kerry coaxed her over and got the paper. It was a photo. It was the family portrait of the Gundersons, the one that had been on the desk in their house!

"How did you get this? I wish you could talk as well as you eat." She wondered if Bubbles had grabbed it before the house was burglarized. She didn't think so, but maybe Koshou had packed it into the girl's bags that first night. Kerry didn't remember unpacking it, but she had been very tired.

She absently put it in the drawer of her night stand and shooed the monkey back out the window. Tightening the belt of her robe, she decided to get breakfast and a cup of tea before getting back into that silly pink dress that seemed to laugh at her from the bed.

Next door, at the school, Minnie heard someone come in the front door. She stuck her head out of her office to see who was there.

"Hello. May I help you?" she asked a young professional man and then did a double take. "Rand, I did not recognize you!"

He stood grinning in the hallway, truly transformed. His hair had been cut very short in the latest, easy-care style. Now, when he combed his fingers through it absent-mindedly, it fell right back into place. In fact, the barber, so pleased to finally get his hands on that mess, had found that Rand's thinning hair was not very difficult to disguise. It was only Rand's home barbering jobs that had made it so apparent. The blond color had always been rich, and sun streaks didn't hurt his coloring either.

Next, Rand had gone to the optometrist, who rose out of his chair in horror when he saw the mangled, out-of-date frames Rand wore. Realizing his customer had been the victim of some vicious attack and was now too shocked to have any opinion of frames, the man took great care in finding the right look. This customer was obviously intelligent and had good, strong brow bones. Now, where was that new shipment from the States?

Rand looked completely different from the neck up when he emerged from the store. Unfortunately, he still looked like his grandpa from the neck down. His new glasses, he thought as he checked them out in the reflection from the window front, reminded him of a professor. A distinguished professor, or maybe a lawyer. He liked that.

Mr. Ramphu, the tailor in the neighborhood, was Minnie's uncle. He had never seen Rand until today and wondered why no one had suggested some new things before now. He couldn't know that Rand had spent many years fending off the suggestions.

When Rand stepped out of his clothing to try on some new slacks and shirts, Mr. Ramphu suggested they start at skin level and brought in three new sets of shorts and undershirts, with the understanding that he was throwing them in as a charitable act.

Rand grumbled and mumbled, blocked the chair against the changing room doorknob, and speedily became presentable on all levels.

In crisp, dark gray slacks, pin-striped shirt with a button-down collar, and a yellow silk tie, Rand walked out of Uncle Ramphu's shop looking like a new person. Having purchased two new suits, a navy double-breasted sport coat, camel slacks, boxes of shirts, five new ties, and even a pair of new blue jeans, he felt he had behaved decadently.

The rest of the clothes were to be delivered that afternoon. He wore a new pair of buttery soft brown loafers and purchased a black pair to go with the suits. No wonder Minnie hardly recognized him!

He'd blown all of his Christmas money from his family, even though Minnie's uncle had given him a break by including the small items free of charge. In previous years he'd spent his Christmas money at the bookstore, his only personal extravagance.

Gwen wandered into the school hallway, on her way to the clinic, and stopped dead. "Rand, you are unbelievably good-looking," she smiled. "Who would have ever guessed?" She continued on her way.

For the next few minutes, students made extra trips into the hallway to see the sight as word spread quickly through the building. Everyone had a comment and they were all positive.

"You are such a surprise!"

"How handsome you are today."

"I really like the outfit."

Rand couldn't wait until he saw Kerry. In fact, after checking himself over one more time in his room, he put on the navy double-breasted blazer, picked up his briefcase, and decided to bowl her over with professionalism. Ha! Tyler wasn't the only spiffy dresser anymore!

And with that kind and neighborly thought, Rand walked over to the Greysons' house to find Danielle and Kathryn in the kitchen making maple buns with Mrs. Peters. All of them had flour up to their elbows, and Kathryn had it all over her face.

Rand cleared his throat.

All three turned and stood speechless for a moment.

Mrs. Peters, grasping the full import of the situation in a second said, "Ho, ho, ho! Fighting fire with fire, are we?"

"Mrs. Peters! Whatever could you mean?" Rand answered with exaggerated politeness.

Kathryn hid her face in Danielle's shoulder. The older girl looked a little puzzled. "Hi, Rand," was all that she said.

"Hi? That's all? No hugs or kisses this morning?"

"We'd mess you up. Where are you going?"

"Well, to tell you the truth, I have some very, very important business to attend to today. I need to have a little chat with Kerry. Is she at home?"

"She's reading the paper in the library."

Mrs. Peters spoke to the air. "I'd rather that they live here, but next door would do, I suppose."

Rand wondered what she was talking about and if any of them had blinked once since he came in the room. He couldn't wait to see Kerry's expression when she saw the new, improved him.

Kerry sat in the library in a wing chair, sipping her cup of tea and reading the English newspaper. Every few minutes she glanced at the beautiful ring. It was so pretty, even if it was an imitation. What a nice thank-you present from Tyler!

Pausing outside the door to adjust his tie, Rand put on his serious, I-have-a-lot-of-important-business face to impress Kerry.

"Miss Carlyle, may I have a moment of your time?"

"Sure, Rand, come on in."

He paused dramatically in the doorway, displaying his new look to full advantage. He waited for the gasp. It didn't come. Kerry still hadn't looked up.

"I wanted to talk to you about the Gundersons and their disappearance," he stated and was pleased to see her look up and notice him finally.

"Oh, good. I've been meaning to tell you about the story that Danielle believes. It might just be a delusion, but what if it's true?"

Was she looking at him? Rand checked. Yes, she was focusing on his face. Maybe she's nearsighted and can't truly see me across the room. I'll get much closer.

"Kerry, do you like my new tie?"

Kerry's brow furrowed at this abrupt change of subject from something important to something trivial. "I'm sorry, Rand, I hadn't noticed. Yes, it's a nice tie. Did you know that Danielle thinks she saw a man pushing her father into a car behind the neighbor's house?"

"Yes!" he answered irritably. "I talked with her at length the other day in my office. I must admit that it would fit with some other evidence I found," and he quickly told her about finding the pen, watch, and ring in the back yard.

"I informed the police, but they didn't seem very interested."

At that moment, the library door opened, and Gwen came in to get some papers from the desk. "Oh, sorry, didn't mean to interrupt!"

"You didn't interrupt anything," Rand growled.

Gwen smiled, "What do you think of Rand's new look, Kerry?"

Kerry looked Rand over more closely. "Why, you do look as though you're going somewhere," she said with some bewilderment. "Are you?"

"Am I what?" he almost yelled.

"Going somewhere?"

"I'm going crazy, want to come?" he said in a disgusted tone.

Gwen broke into giggles and quickly left. Kerry wondered if all the strain had finally unhinged Rand.

"You know, Rand, the girls and I were going to the market later on. Maybe you should take a break from the school and come with us. Relax a little. Take it easy. Have fun."

"I'm having fun right now!" he snarled.

"Well, you seem annoyed to me, but I don't know you that well."

"And just what would it take for you to get to know me *that* well, Kerry?" he demanded, leaning over and grabbing both of her hands. "What do you think of me?" he asked very intently.

Kerry wondered where this was going. "I think you're a nice man who wants to help people."

"That's not what I mean! How do I look to you? Let's

say I wanted to look more attractive to a young lady, whom I will not name. Do you think I might achieve that aim?"

Gwen, Kerry thought. How awful to have to be the guinea pig. "No," she answered pointedly.

"No? Never? I'm just too ugly for words, or what?"

"You asked if you could look 'more' attractive. You're already an attractive man. Especially when you're in the middle of a project or intent on something that you feel is important. People follow your leadership and honor your walk with God. You care about your patients and your students, and I don't think you can improve on that by looking prettier," Kerry said in a matter-of-fact way. What was his problem this morning?

"Men do not want to look prettier," was his answer.

Rand stepped back. He'd been complimented. Of course, it wasn't exactly what he'd been expecting. In fact, come to think of it, it didn't sound as if she had any interest in him at all, other than as a fellow humanitarian. Arrrgh!

He had been such a ninny to kiss her last night. She's probably trying to keep me at arm's length, he concluded. "Er . . . about last night in the kitchen. I wanted to apologize."

He's sorry he kissed me, Kerry concluded. She smiled stiffly. She wanted to go through the floor. Instead, she looked at her emerald ring and felt much better. "I'd already forgotten."

Great day! She'd forgotten? He couldn't think of anything else, and she'd forgotten?

"Rand, what are you going to do about the Gundersons?"

144

"I'm not able to do a thing about the Gundersons," he answered, frustrated beyond measure. "I am only one man, who feels all his responsibilities and frustrations far too heavily today!" Rand grimly announced as he stood to leave. "Let's eat dinner out tonight," he nearly demanded.

"I'm sorry, Rand, but I'm having dinner with Tyler," Kerry said quickly, wondering if he meant to go out to the village again.

When he got to the door, he turned to look back on Kerry's wide-eyed stare. "I would love to go to the market with you and the children this afternoon. I want to relax, have fun, and stop radiating strength and honor! Come and get me when you're ready!" he almost shouted, glaring at Kerry and slamming the door behind him.

Kerry let out a long "whew."

The phone in the library rang. Mrs. Peters came in to answer it. "Miss Carlyle, it's for you."

Kerry ran to get it. She'd been waiting in the library for the return call from Mr. Miller. She closed the door so that no one would overhear her side of the conversation.

"Oh, hello, sir. You were able to check those things out? Yes? Yes? So there was a soil core report done? On both? Really. You don't have a copy per chance? Just the one?

"What about the trust and children? Does he have a good chance? Well, yes, they seem to like him quite a lot. The home is very nice. Mrs. Peters? Lovely, you couldn't get anyone better.

"So we still need to come back to the States for the court to make the decisions and appointments? Yes, well, I was thinking that the girls should stay with me while that's happening. After all, they're used to me, and I hate to cause yet more upheaval in their lives.

"Oh, good, that's a relief. Yes, day after tomorrow. Yes, yes! It will be good to be back," Kerry said without much enthusiasm.

She hung up, very distracted. The information was irrelevant at best. Kerry felt depressed by the immediate plans to return to the United States.

She wondered if Rand was going to ask Gwen to marry him. It made her choke to think he'd asked her how he could be more attractive for Gwen. And he was afraid she'd take that little kitchen scene seriously. Ha! He'd soon realize that his little peck on her cheek meant nothing.

Kerry looked angry as she ran upstairs to get dressed for the day. She grimaced when she looked at the wrinkle-free dress de jour. Why had she thought they were so nifty, and why did she buy three of them? It sounded well and good never to worry about looking wrinkled, but at the end of the day your clothes ought to look as tired as you are. Otherwise, they just emphasized your tired face without looking as though you'd earned that face through hard work!

Come to think of it, Kerry couldn't ever remember Tyler looking rumpled, sweaty, or even tired. What did he do all day?

Picking up the hot pink number with pastel parrots, the dress she'd worn the least, Kerry slipped it over her head and let the fabric settle around her. Now, this hair!

Kerry, wanting to stay cool at the market, braided her low ponytail tightly and looped it into a knot at her neck, anchoring it with two big pins. Then she went in search of Mrs. Peters.

"Would you mind if I borrowed your gardening hat. I'm breaking out into freckles, and I don't want to be too red for tonight's fancy dinner with Tyler."

Mrs. Peters laughed and fetched a broad straw hat that had bright straw fruit embroidered all over the crown like some Carmen Miranda production. A bouncy fringe of colored straw balls decorated the brim to frighten flies away. When she plunked it on Kerry's head, they broke into giggles.

"Well, Miss Carlyle, if they don't see you coming in that colorful get-up, they must be blind."

"I do look a bit gaudy and festive, don't I?"

"I know just the perfect addition," Mrs. Peters said over her shoulder as she went into another room and came back with an oversized straw purse covered with more straw fruit and the pièce de résistance, a pair of big pink sunglasses with bananas painted on the corners!

"Oh, they're wonderful!"

Danielle and Kathryn danced around her as if she were a maypole and begged to buy hats for themselves along with their shoes. The party mood was upon them in full force, and the girls went up to get ready for the expedition.

They couldn't find any straw hats, but they did find some old party hats from the pantry, which they wore with panache.

It was with some trepidation that Minnie called up to Rand to tell him that his friends were waiting. He'd shrugged out of his jacket but still looked impeccable in his slacks, shirt, and tie. He grabbed his wallet, came down the stairs, and felt as though he had walked into a parade.

Kathryn and Danielle were having a hopping contest, bouncing around the foyer, while Kerry picked up the contents of her purse, which she'd accidentally dumped on the floor.

It was a very colorful and active group. When Rand bent down to examine the woman under the hat and shades, he recognized the freckles on the nose and that was about all.

"I see that I have been given a great honor to escort the most cheerful, fashionable women in New Delhi today," he said, feeling much better. This group was crazy, but he liked it.

Just then, they heard someone clear his throat from the doorway. Rand, Kerry, Minnie, and the girls turned around to hear Mr. Hansa Rupa Das from the state department say, "I'm not interrupting anything, am I?"

# TWELVE

**RAND COULDN'T HAVE** planned it any better.

Mr. Hansa Rupa Das could never have interpreted those outfits as anything dangerous or threatening to the neighborhood. Rand shook the official's hand and begged his pardon, explaining that they were having a special outing and these children could not be denied their fun.

They left Mr. Rupa Das shaking his head in wonderment as they walked down to the market.

The first important task was to buy Danielle a big pair of green sunglasses with sparkles on the corners and Kathryn a large hat with a straw parrot perched on top.

Kerry looked at Rand, who was buying balloons, and thought he would make a very good father. Of course, he did look a little too straitlaced in that outfit. She hurried over and bought him a tall straw hat with a straw monkey hanging onto the pointed crown.

"Rand?" she held the hat behind her, "would you bend down and close your eyes, please?" she asked sweetly, smiling.

Rand obediently, expectantly, hopefully, bent down to lip level and found himself wearing a profoundly ugly hat.

Kerry and the children laughed.

"Just for that, I am going to insist on wearing it all day, and do not be surprised if people think that we are the circus, newly arrived."

They all linked arms and moved on to get lunch and snacks from the many stands along the way.

The sun was very hot and quickly depleted their energy.

After purchasing black canvas Mary Janes for the girls, they found some seats under a banyan tree for shade and a little rest. Kerry felt very tired. The girls found it quite natural to pile against Rand. He easily accommodated them, his arms stretched on the back of the park bench. Kathryn put her head on his chest and immediately closed her eyes for a nap. Even Danielle was quiet and still, leaning against Rand's left side. Kerry was trying to resist putting her own head against his shoulder when he reached over, his own eyes shaded, and pulled her hat off.

"Kerry, relax," he mumbled, closing his eyes.

Kerry gave into temptation and found a comfortable place, leaning her face against his outstretched arm, and promptly fell into a deep sleep.

That was how Koshou found them all when she went to buy vegetables for her family's supper. She stood in front of the group, wondering if they'd been to a carnival. Just then, Danielle woke up, recognized her, and gave a cry of surprise.

Koshou was so happy to see her girls! There were hugs all around. She said that they were exactly the people she wanted to see!

"I know you are getting ready to leave in a few days.

I was going to try and call you this evening. My family would like to invite you for a big meal tomorrow night. We will miss the little ones so much, and perhaps you would enjoy something different."

Kerry and Rand accepted with alacrity, and it took promises of sweets to pull the children away from Koshou. Rand took them for the promised candy while Kerry went into a shop to buy her saris. Rand said he would be back in time to dicker for her.

Kerry wandered among the tables and shelves. One display, a white silk shot through with gold threads and embroidery, kept catching her eye. It was lovely, for a very special occasion, no doubt. Maybe a wedding?

Kerry tried to decide between a brilliant green length of material and a pastel pink.

Rand came up behind her. He touched the green material first. "This one reminds me of you when your eyes sparkle and you're angry," he laughed. Then he touched the softer pink, adding, "But this one reminds me of you when you're relaxed and cooking."

Kerry felt distracted as Rand looked at her an overly long moment. She knew that he was complimenting her, and it upset her. She didn't want him to know that his charming comments could affect her.

She dropped the material and moved to another table with different types of cloth. Rand followed her and pointed to the white with gold thread that she'd admired earlier. "I think you would be very beautiful in that sari." He smiled at her and then moved away to check on the children, who were playing hide and seek in the store.

Kerry wondered if anyone would notice if she fainted on the table. Release your breath, now bring another one in. How could he do that? He hadn't said anything remotely romantic, and here she was, her face burning bright, her vision blurry, and her knees as weak as water.

She went back to the first table and picked up the green material, holding onto it like a lifejacket. And indeed, she felt as if she were drowning. And then, ignoring all logic, she picked up the pink material and finally the white and gold bolt, which was far too expensive.

Putting all three on the counter, she went to find Rand and the girls, who were playing hide and seek among the wares. "Would you help me make my purchase now?"

Rand's eyebrows rose when he saw her choices. "My favorites? You shouldn't have, Kerry," he teased her.

She felt like kicking him in the shins but couldn't in front of young, impressionable minds.

Walking back home, with everyone carrying bundles, they paused to look into the window of a brass shop. Suddenly, Kathryn put her head back and wailed, loud enough to get everyone's attention, "Mommy!"

Danielle took off running in the direction that Kathryn pointed, Rand right on her heels. Kerry picked up the sobbing child and followed the others, her purchases swinging and flapping.

A large group of women in dark *burkhas* turned to see Rand and Danielle running after them and took off in fear, screaming. They scattered like chickens. Rand, Danielle, and finally Kerry, who was still carrying Kathryn, stopped. Out of breath and unsure of where to run next, they stood panting.

"Did you see anything?" Rand asked Danielle. She was crying now, the tears silently running down her face. She shook her head negatively.

Kathryn was still calling, "Mommy!" but had her head on Kerry's shoulder. Rand reached over and pulled Danielle into the group. All the ladies had a good cry, while Rand held them and looked grim.

By the time they got home, Kathryn was asleep, Rand carrying her. Danielle was leaning on Kerry. Mrs. Peters took one look at the rag-tag bunch and put the children to bed without asking any questions. Kerry sat in the library, too tired to move, while Rand perched on the arm of a chair.

"I just wish I knew what triggers that in Kathryn. What does she see?" he asked a painting on the wall.

Kerry just shook her head, deeply disturbed. "Rand, why did the women run?"

"It is the custom of *purdah* to keep the women separate and hidden from all men except their father, husband, or brother. *Purdah* was brought to India by the Muslim invaders, and many Hindus adopted the custom. Today, only the more orthodox groups still observe it so rigidly."

There were so many pieces of this puzzle, but Kerry didn't seem to be able to put them together! Looking down, she noticed the emerald ring again, but this time it just looked as dark and as opaque as her thoughts. To crown the whole situation, her rotten ear was starting to ache and throb, adding a special touch of misery to an already depressed spirit.

"Rand, I'm sorry everything turned into a mess. You keep getting roped into this, when you have your own worries."

Rand looked at Kerry long and thoughtfully. Then he walked over and pulled her up by her hand until she was standing. "What's the matter?" he asked.

"Everything's the matter."

"I mean, what hurts? Remember, I'm a doctor. It's fairly obvious that you're in some kind of pain."

"I have a miserable ear."

"You look like you need a rest before your big evening," he said gently. "I'll get my bag and come back to look at your ear before you go. I don't want you to be miserable all night," he added.

Nodding, Kerry left the room. She walked woodenly up the stairs.

Rand watched until she was gone and then went back to the school. He thought he might make some very important calls that afternoon.

Kerry walked sadly up to the nursery and looked in on the sleeping girls. They were so undeserving of the upheaval in their lives.

Bubbles the monkey was on Danielle's bed, where she didn't belong, but Kerry didn't have the heart to move her. She was playing with something. Kerry reached over to see what it was and was surprised to find a passport. She opened it, afraid that Bubbles had gotten into her purse, but it belonged to Mrs. Gunderson. Now, how did she get that? Kerry knew that she had never packed any passports but the children's on that first night. Frowning, she took it from the monkey and carried it over to the dresser, where she'd put the family photo of the Gundersons.

This photo, in typical passport style, was not very flattering, but Mrs. Gunderson looked like a nice person, with smiling eyes and a crooked grin. Danielle was going to look a great deal like her someday.

Somehow, it just depressed Kerry all the more. How

could anyone deliberately break up a family? She didn't believe those parents had abandoned Danielle and Kathryn. Those children were too warm and well-adjusted not to have been very loved.

Rand must have brought the "Travel" file, family photo, and other desk papers with him.

"Bubbles, are you stealing things from his office?" she asked the unrepentant monkey. "I'll ask him."

The monkey curled into a ball on the blanket and closed her eyes to take a nap.

Glancing around her room, Kerry realized that it was quite large and very lovely. The whole house was very comfortable. Kerry had lived in several comfortable apartments on the East Coast, but nothing as grand as this house.

When Kerry was a little girl, she used to wish that when she woke up in the morning, her room would become a princess's room. It was too bad she couldn't make that dream come true for those poor, disappointed darlings.

She put her hand to her throbbing ear and lay down on her bed, pushing Bubbles off. Her eyes closed, but in prayer, not sleep.

She quietly told God how confused and sad she was feeling. She talked to Him sincerely, without flowery words or phrases. She could feel her tension unwind and leave her as she passed her problems into His hands.

Finally, she dozed off, a relaxed look to her face. She only slept a few minutes but felt much better when she awoke.

Stretching, Kerry reached up and bumped into the mosquito netting hanging over her bed. A wonderful thought occurred to her, and the mosquito netting was just the beginning!

She ran downstairs, her tiredness gone, and found Mrs. Peters. After quickly relaying their awful experience at the market, she shared her brilliant idea, and minutes later the two women were bumping around in the storage closets, finding all sorts of castaways. They brought out bolts of mosquito netting, thin wire, snips, and some old beads that one of Tyler's sisters had left on a visit many years ago.

Working silently so as not to wake the room's occupants, they stood on chairs and worked as quickly as they dared in the nursery. Eventually Kerry ran down to the living room, bringing up all the throw pillows, and scattered them around. Mrs. Peters brought up a great tray of cookies and lemonade and set it in the middle of the floor.

"Wake up, princesses!" she called softly. Both girls opened their eyes and found that they sat in a rajah's palace! The netting was anchored on the ceiling light fixture and created a soft, cloudy tent. The beads lay piled in an old music box, like a treasure chest, and there presiding over the tray of cookies sat a very exotic lady, covered in saris and scarves, with only her eyes peeking out.

"Come my leetle royal children," said the heavily accented voice, which sounded like a combination of Romanian royalty and Italian peasantry to Mrs. Peters. "You must prepare for this wonderful banquet!"

Kerry clapped her hands and beckoned them closer. "Wherrrre," rolled her tongue, "are your beautiful clothes?" she asked the amazed faces.

Mrs. Peters held up the box of charity things and said, "I think I've found them, Your Supreme Highnesses."

Tyler came wandering upstairs to see where everyone had gone. He followed the squeals of delight and found a virtual harem in his house. Danielle and Kathryn were covered from head to foot in flowing garments.

He quickly went to the bathroom, got a towel, and made himself a turban. Reentering with a swagger, he bellowed, "The sultan has returned! Where are the beautiful girls that wait on me?" His accent was decidedly Russian.

Both children ran and bowed down very low. He sat down cross-legged next to Kerry, tweaked her veil aside, and whispered in her ear. "I hate to drag you away, but our reservations at the club are for one hour from now. May I fill in for your loveliness, while you change?"

Kerry had completely forgotten about their dinner, she was so caught up in the palace preparations! "Oh, Tyler, thank you. I lost track of time."

"Well, I can see why, creating a harem to surprise me," Tyler teased, wagging his eyebrows comically. He caught her hand before she stood up and pulled her closer, whispering in her ear, "I know you'll be beautiful tonight."

Kerry laughed. "Don't you want me to wear this outfit to the club, Tyler? Do I look too realistic in my seven veils?"

Kerry closed the door that joined her room to the nursery and quickly stepped out of the exotic finery. Wrapping her robe around her, she ran down the hall, took a quick shower, and washed her hair. She would be utterly sophisticated tonight, just to show Tyler how much she appreciated his putting up with all of them in his home this past week.

Patting on L'Heure Bleu dusting powder, layering it with some spritzes of the same scent in cologne, and even adding a drop of the bath oil behind each ear, Kerry decided that she would last, scentwise, throughout the evening.

She put on the one black dress that she had packed, which was very simple but had cost a whole week's salary, even on sale. Her mother claimed that she could be buried in it someday, because it would never go out of style. The quality showed in the way that it fit, emphasizing her lovely throat. The scalloped black neckline made her face look sculptured. The sleeves tapered to right below the elbow.

Kerry slipped on black silk stockings and was glad she had included a pair of strapped black heels in that wonderful carry-on bag.

Now, the hair. It was almost dry. Kerry fluffed the front and wrapped the rest into a smooth French twist. She looked elegant and chic.

Finally, assembling a few coins (a habit she would never outgrow), a hankie, and small compact, she realized that she had no evening bag to carry. Well, maybe she wouldn't carry anything.

Kerry opened the door to the nursery and found that Tyler and Mrs. Peters were gone, leaving the children to continue their play. Both children oooohed when they saw her.

"You look beautiful," Danielle supplied.

"Like Mommy," Kathryn added, starting to speak more often in Kerry's presence.

"Yeah, you look like Mom when she's going out to dinner with Dad."

Kerry was afraid that memory would set off unhappy emotions and waited with held breath, but the girls continued with their make-believe kingdom business. She kissed them both and gave them each a spritz of perfume, telling them that they could be very elegant ladies this evening along with her.

She walked back through her room to check the window, and there on her dresser was a bunch of flowers. They looked like orchids, but not orchids that Kerry had ever seen before. They were pale blue, with deeper blue veins and mottled centers. They were delicate and lovely. There were five of them on a stem, and each one was as big as the palm of her hand. Tyler must have put them here, Kerry thought. They would go perfectly with her dress.

Kerry pinned them into her hair. How special they were!

Then remembering something, Kerry went to her luggage, and started throwing things out of her carry-on bag onto her bed, frantically digging in all the pockets.

"Aha!" she cried, holding up a pale blue silk scarf, exactly the same hue as her flowers. Laying the square on the bed, she gathered her change, compact, and hankie and put them in the middle of the scarf. Then she loosely tied her possessions into a tiny hobo's sack, held it like an evening bag and let the long ends of the scarf trail, gently fluttering as she walked.

Kerry stopped at the top of the staircase. Rand stood talking to Tyler at the bottom. What was he doing there? Oh, he wanted to look at her ear.

She began to walk down when Rand noticed her, broke off his sentence, and just stared.

Tyler began to clap and say, "Bravo! You will be the hit of the club. Every man there shall envy me tonight. I knew you would be stunning in a sophisticated atmosphere but, my dear, this is beyond my expectations. I am the luckiest man alive!"

He rushed up the stairs to take her hand, checking it for the emerald. "And you honor me so by wearing the family emerald tonight, sweet delight! You know, it was my grandmother's and then my mother's ring."

Rand still said not one word. He watched Kerry's face intently, never breaking eye contact for a moment.

"Is it official, then, Tyler?" he quietly asked.

"Well, I hope so, but then I won't push this exquisite piece of beauty, lest she break. Perhaps we can make some sort of announcement before you leave, Kerry, my lovely?"

Kerry was drowning in Rand's eyes and hadn't caught any of their conversation. Her bad ear was stopped up, and the good ear was on the wrong side to pick up their comments.

Rand cleared his throat. "Maybe I can quickly look at your ear in the library before you go."

"Of course," she agreed.

Tyler, feeling that he was somehow losing ground here, accompanied them and sat next to Kerry, almost hampering the exam.

Rand tried to avoid touching her and hurriedly gave her some drops and pills.

Tyler almost pulled Kerry out the front door and put her into the front seat of an unusual little red car.

"I couldn't resist buying something special today for such a special evening. This is India's Ambassador, modeled after the 1950s British Morris Oxford. It would make a nice engagement present, yes?" he asked Kerry, not waiting for an answer, patting her cheek and then walking around to the other side.

It never registered with Kerry. All she could see was Rand standing on the verandah, arms crossed, disproving glare, eyes boring into her soul. It distracted her to no end and made her want to hide. How dare he ruin her lovely evening! She would just show him! She'd have the most wonderful time imaginable. With effort, Kerry focused her attention on Tyler's amusing stories, laughing a little too hard.

Over dinner that evening, in the all-white Royal Asiatic Club, Kerry found her mind wandering. The food was only fair, and the service very poor.

"Thank you, Tyler, for the beautiful flowers. I've never seen anything like them."

"I'm delighted that they suit you so well. They are blue vanda orchids, discovered by Dr. Griffith in Assam over one hundred years ago. They're one of the first blue orchids ever discovered by the Western scientific world."

Tyler was entertaining in his own way, and without warning he dropped the bombshell. "You know, Kerry, I am offering Rand a handsome profit for the school."

"What?"

"Yes, he's always had to scrape to meet the notes, and now that the neighborhood has turned against him I thought he might like to start again in a different area, maybe the northeastern part of India."

"I wasn't aware that he was thinking of moving the school and clinic," Kerry responded, disturbed for some unknown reason.

"Yes, well, Gwen is thinking of relocating, and you know, she is the one who originally brought Rand and the development of the medical program to New Delhi."

"Perhaps they mentioned it," Kerry responded very faintly.

"Anyway, I've offered them almost twice what they've paid on it, plus picking up the rest of the mortgage. That's enough profit to start a better place somewhere else."

"Oh, I see."

"Which brings me to another subject. With Gwen leaving and the possibility of Kathryn and Danielle coming to be my wards, Mrs. Peters and I will be very lonely without you. Would you consider having me, an old man, as your husband?"

Tyler knew that he had never looked better and often used the phrase "old man" as a contrast to his movie-star looks.

Reaching across the table to hold Kerry's hand, he looked deeply and sincerely into her eyes.

Kerry almost choked.

She had not seen this coming. Why not? It had been obvious from the first that Tyler found her attractive. Goodness knows, he'd been the only one to lavish compliments on her.

It would be the answer to many problems. She could stay with the children, she liked Mrs. Peters, and Tyler was handsome and rich. Actually it solved everybody's problems, didn't it? Gwen would be moving away . . . with Rand. Kerry looked down at the beautiful emerald ring on her hand. It simply glowed in the club's light. Tyler hadn't mentioned that it belonged in his family when he gave it to her. It must be real, after all. She loathed taking it off.

"Tyler, this is so . . . sudden."

"Well, I will not rush you, sweet child. But please consider my offer. I can think of nothing that would bring me more pleasure than to have a family again. And with Gwen leaving, you would have the whole house to redecorate, however you wished. And twice a year, you will go to Europe with me to refurbish yours and the children's wardrobes from the most famous designers on earth."

Tyler felt a bit like twirling his imaginary villain's mustache.

# THIRTEEN

**LATE THAT NIGHT,** after getting back from the club, Tyler put his arms around Kerry in a quick hug and wished her peaceful dreams. Unfortunately, Kerry couldn't get to sleep.

The night was chilly for India, but a comfortable forty degrees for Kerry. She wrapped one of Gwen's robes from the guest closet around her and stared out of her window down to the garden. It was beautiful in the moonlight. If she lived here, it could be hers. Even this room might be hers. Well . . . no. She'd have a room with Tyler, on the other side of the house.

Kerry's ear ached at the thought. Maybe her future daughter-in-law, Gwen, should check it. Maybe Rand would become her son-in-law, and she would start calling him "Sonny," and his children would call her "Grandma." And maybe the funny farm had a room with her name on it.

On the other hand, did she want to go back to the States and her lonely existence there? It hadn't seemed lonely a week ago. Now, she could hardly bear the thought of going back. Wouldn't it be lovely not to worry about money anymore?

Kerry's mind debated the issue back and forth, cold logic at war with emotionalism.

She did not pray. She did not want to, because she knew that she was contemplating marriage to a man who had no active relationship with God (not that she held the Olympic record for continuous communication herself).

Had Tyler said that he loved her? Did she love him? Was it even necessary? They got along quite well. After all, they never argued, unlike some others she could name.

She was lucky to get Tyler. Wouldn't her friends at home be impressed when she sent pictures? He was so handsome and distinguished, with prestige in the community. No one dropped bombs in his yard. He was doing something to help employ locals, not change them.

Kerry finally talked herself into accepting Tyler's offer after the banquet at Koshou's. Then they could announce it to the children, and it would be a happy ending to the day.

Kerry shrugged off the recent recommitment that she'd made to God, ignoring the sudden weight in her heart. Her Bible was open on her bed, but Kerry closed it and put it away, promising herself that she'd try to read it tomorrow.

With that thought, Kerry lay down and drifted into a nightmare.

She dreamed that she was working at the shoe factory and that huge bloody hides kept piling up in front of her, but she didn't know what to do and couldn't keep up. Rand and Gwen came past her laughing, but she was trapped under the hides.

Then Danielle and Kathryn were playing in the equipment, near dangerous parts, getting closer and closer to whirling sharp blades. They couldn't hear Kerry's screams telling them to watch and be careful.

Finally Tyler came out of his office, holding that soil report and telling her that he'd found beryl, but Kerry couldn't quite understand why that was important. He just laughed and said that she didn't have to worry about anything anymore. He was taking care of all of them.

Kerry tossed and moaned and woke the next morning exhausted, frustrated, and feeling very confused.

After picking at her breakfast and finding that the children were going to visit the elephant, Kerry wandered around the Greysons' house. It was lovely, and there were only a few changes that Kerry would make. Maybe some new drapes and a few rearranged items of furniture. Maybe not.

Tyler was at the factory, Gwen had gone out to a village, and Mrs. Peters was working in her herb garden, so Kerry wandered over to the Bible school.

She immediately sensed a buzz in the air. No one was in class, and many were speaking in whispers in small groups. Rand stood in the main office, staring into space in a distracted sort of way.

"Hello. What's going on?" Kerry interrupted his thoughts.

Rand jumped at the sound of her voice. "It appears we have been formally challenged," he explained.

"One of our neighborhood gurus sent a messenger with an open invitation to war, tomorrow, at daybreak."

"What?"

"Yes, it seems that with the *maha kumbh mela* so close in time, the local Hindus are feeling more confident of their powers and have decided to show the neighborhood, once and for all, who's boss."

"Has this ever happened before?"

Now Rand smiled. "I think Elijah used to have some confrontations of this variety," he announced ironically.

"Stop that!" Kerry frowned. "This is serious."

"Yes, it is serious."

"What are you going to do?"

"Well, I'm not sure what we are precisely going to do, but I can guess at the Hindus. Considering the reputation of their *fakirs* and the embrace of demons in their religion, I'd guess they plan to scare us away and their own people into obedience. Make sure the children are safely indoors with Mrs. Peters in the morning. I wouldn't want anything to frighten them, more than they've already had in their lives."

Kerry nodded in agreement. "Is there anything we can do?"

"Oh, yes, I would ask you to stay out of the way, Miss Carlyle," Rand said, reverting to the formal title.

"Can't you tell them that you're getting ready to leave and that this won't be a Bible school or a clinic anymore?"

That gained Rand's complete attention. He grabbed her shoulders and spoke harshly. "I am only here on a tourist's visa, Miss Carlyle, but I am not aware that the Bible school or medical clinic is getting ready to go somewhere. I will say it again. Stay out of the way. I cannot risk anyone using you to get to me," he added brusquely and walked away.

Of course not, Kerry thought. Here I am, in the way again. He must hate me.

Kerry walked out of the office and saw the latest bit of

vandalism in the back courtyard. Garbage had been strewn all over. Students were trying to pick it up, but they had at least an hour's worth of work out there. Kerry hurried out to help them.

Rand sat in his office and felt angry. He was angry because Tyler was offering him a sweet way to get rid of his responsibilities, and it appealed too much.

How tempting it would be to pack it all in and go back to the States on the same plane as Kerry, Danielle, and Kathryn! And yet, he started this whole show, and they surely needed him now. He also felt that something in the Gundersons' disappearance wasn't resolved. Unfortunately, the police weren't interested, and he wasn't getting anywhere. They had received no ransom demands, so where were they? The Gundersons hadn't taken any money from Geraghty and Miller. Their bank accounts were still modest and untouched since their disappearance.

And just what exactly was going on between Tyler and Kerry? Rand wasn't getting clear signals in anything these days!

Rand asked God, in a conversational tone, if He happened to be noticing how wretched Rand's life was quickly becoming.

That evening found them all dressed in their best for dinner with Koshou's family.

In Tyler's car, with the children sitting on Rand and Gwen's lap in the back seat, the six set out. Gwen looked cool and collected in a plain linen shift and coral-colored loose jacket. Rand had dressed in one of his new suits and occasionally pulled on the neck of the shirt as though his tie bothered him. Tyler was impeccable in a

raw silk jacket, dark pants, white shirt, and brightly pat-
terned tie. The children wore their parachute dresses
along with their new socks and Mary Jane shoes.

Only Kerry had decided against Western clothing and
wore her new deep green sari, anchoring it with safety
pins, and her loose white silk shirt underneath. Her outfit
matched the emerald on her finger, which she twisted ner-
vously. One finger absently traced the elephant carved
into the gold setting. Elephants were lucky, weren't they?

She remembered her conversation with Rand, when
he'd asked her if she would rather entrust her future to
luck and chance or a loving God.

In her hair she had woven some of the jasmine vine
from the backyard, and she felt somewhat clearer of mind
when she smelled its fragrance. She knew that she did not
want to leave that sweet smell. She also hated to go back
to Western clothes, never having another chance to wear
the comfortable sari back in Ohio.

Only Danielle talked much during the ride. Tyler
seemed preoccupied, and Rand was very tense. Gwen was
busy playing patty-cake with Kathryn. Kerry was so ner-
vous that she made an effort to think about something
unimportant.

She imagined herself coming to a neighborhood Ohio
barbecue in her sari. She knew Earl and Flo next door
would probably drop their spatulas, while every kid on
the block would try and unwrap her. Kerry bit back giggles, the strain of everything beginning to show.

Of course, she wouldn't be back in Ohio very long.
Tyler would expect her to marry him pretty soon, she
would imagine. Would she marry him in her church?
Would he be the same age as her father? She'd never actu-

ally asked him how old he was. Maybe he was a young seventy. She looked over at his perfect profile and wondered.

Rand watched as Kerry seemed to find endless fascination in gazing at Tyler's face. She hadn't even noticed him with new clothes, new glasses, and a new haircut. He mauled his tie some more.

Tyler knew that Kerry found him handsome. Why, just look at the way she was studying him! He pretended he didn't notice. He just hoped the wind from the open window wasn't blowing his hair off that little thinning spot in the back. That's why he always made Gwen sit behind him in a group, so no one else would see.

Gwen, the only untroubled soul in the car, wondered if she could remember all the words to "Pop Goes the Weasel" and plunged back into a variation of patty-cake.

Once they arrived at Koshou's home, the men and women separated, following the old custom. Tyler and Rand joined the men, Koshou invited Kerry and Gwen to watch the cooking, and the children played with all Koshou's nieces and nephews.

Before entering the kitchen, which was not really attached to the house, Gwen and Kerry had to wash their hands, arms, and faces. And even then, they would only be watching the process from behind a counter, not actually touching the food. Hindu kitchens border on being antiseptically clean, and non-Hindus are not allowed into the cooking area.

Koshou's mother, Mrs. Jagasia, nodded and smiled. She was the matriarch, and it was she who cooked the main vegetarian dishes, while Koshou, her sisters, and sisters-in-law did side dishes.

Kerry watched as Koshou made the *kesar chaval*, or saffron rice. First Koshou poured about two cups of *basumati* rice into a colander set in a large pot of cold water. Then she rubbed the grains lightly between her palms in a washing motion. She changed the water four or five times until the water remained perfectly clear.

Then she placed some saffron threads in a bowl and poured a little boiling water over them. The water turned bright yellow.

Meanwhile, in a heavy copper pan that was coated in silver she poured in about half a cup of *ghee*, or clarified butter, a stick of cinnamon, four whole cloves, and a cup of finely chopped onions.

Cooking the onions until they were clear, she added the drained rice and fried it till it turned golden brown. Then Koshou added water until its level was one knuckle of her forefinger above the rice. "That is always the correct amount," she told Kerry, who hoped her own knuckle would not fail her.

To the water she added a tablespoon of *jaggery* (which looked like a very dark brown sugar), salt, and a few cardamom seeds and brought the whole thing to a boil. Then she dumped in the saffron threads in their yellow water, reduced the heat, and covered the pan with a tight lid.

The meal's menu also included curried cauliflower, yogurt with eggplant, hot curried potatoes, red kidney beans, and a mint chutney. One sister had the full-time job of preparing the *phulkas*, which were whole-wheat, puffed bread circles.

Gwen could converse a bit in Hindi, but Kerry found herself just nodding and smiling. Apparently, Koshou's sister, who was a teacher, did not live in this household. She must live in her husband's family home, Kerry guessed.

Several women kept passing back and forth, in and out of the kitchen, and finally Kerry realized that the men were already eating! In this home, the men ate first and then the women. How frustrating, when she was so hungry.

Finally, when empty platters began to come back, the mother gave her daughters a signal, and they began to fill their own *thalis*. Koshou prepared one for Gwen and one for Kerry.

Mrs. Jagasia touched Kerry's sari and immediately found the safety pins. Laughing, and nodding her approval over the material of the sari, she unwound the cloth and rewrapped it, snugly, with great expertise. Kerry felt as if she were in the hands of her own mother. She never asked permission either to adjust anything she felt was amiss. It must be a "mother thing."

The sisters all giggled, and one ran out and came back with a little compact. It held a red makeup, and she took great delight in giving Kerry a *tika*, or *cum-cum*, the little red spot between the eyebrows used in Hindu circles. She offered to put kohl around her eyes, but Kerry declined, thinking the spot quite exotic enough for her pale face.

For dessert they had *gajar halva*, a sweet carrot dish. Koshou explained that about a pound of shredded carrots were brought to a boil in more than a quart of goat's milk, then cooked over reduced heat for an hour. A cup of dark, sweet *jaggery*, a half of cup of white sugar, two cups of pulverized almonds, and a little ghee were mixed in.

173

Kerry wished she had something to write the recipe on. She'd never remember it.

"Finally, when the *halva* mixture is thick enough to draw away from the sides and bottom of the saucepan in a solid mass, mix a pinch of cardamom seeds, rolled in a kitchen towel and crushed with a rolling pin. The whole mixture is then turned out, onto a large platter. Everyone takes turns sticking toasted pistachios and slivers of toasted almonds into the pudding until it looks like a pin cushion."

The ladies were enjoying themselves, but Rand and Tyler were not having such a wonderful visit.

Tyler hated all this ethnic bother. Give him a British meal anytime. He couldn't understand half of what these fellows were saying, and he wasn't sure they had anything in common anyway.

Rand was miserable because he wanted to get back to the school, he wanted to speak with Kerry alone, and he wanted to find out just what Tyler had up his sleeve.

"Tyler," he said in an aside, after several polite but formal conversations with Mr. Jagasia, "your offer for the school was so unexpected yesterday. I was amazed when Kerry mentioned it this afternoon. I wasn't aware that you'd spoken to anyone else about the offer."

Tyler slapped him on the back and said, "You can't keep important things like that away from someone you plan to spend your life with, my good man."

"You and Kerry are truly engaged?" Rand almost yelped, unaware that one of Mr. Jagasia's younger sons was quietly interpreting this interesting conversation to the vast entertainment of all the men present. They watched like spectators at a soccer match.

"Well, not officially, but I've offered, and she is wearing my emerald. I hope she will let me announce it tonight. You know, I'll probably be named Danielle and Kathryn's guardian, since I'm setting up a trust for their education," Tyler added pompously.

All the men switched their attention from Tyler to Rand, waiting for the reaction. They got it.

Quietly but with sarcasm Rand said, "I suppose there are very few people or things left that your money cannot buy, eh, Tyler?"

Tyler only looked at him, not being very good with comebacks.

Rand stood and bowed to Mr. Jagasia, thanking him formally for a beautiful, delicious dinner, and said goodbye. Before a response could be made, he was gone.

One of the younger sons ran out after him to offer a ride home. That left Tyler alone with the men of the family, every eye in the room resting on him. He squirmed, wondering if anyone spoke English.

"I say, where have the girls got to?"

Mr. Jagasia stood with great dignity, did a half bow, and left the room. At that signal, the younger brothers and sons hustled Tyler out into the foyer, rounded up the children, and brought the ladies for a rather hurried exit.

Tyler never told Gwen or Kerry what had really happened. He told them that Rand was concerned about the school and decided to leave early. Privately, he wondered how Rand got home.

Pulling up outside the Greysons' home, Kerry and Tyler both looked toward the school and noticed Rand's office light. They moved without conversation into the Greysons' foyer.

Gwen pulled off her sandals, yawned, and wished them all a good night's rest, going off to her bed.

Tyler turned to Kerry and pulled her into his arms. "Look, my lovely child, say that you'll never leave, and anything you want is yours."

Kerry's mind, forever playing tricks on her, seemed to hear her mother's voice telling her never to accept toys and sweets from strange men. The ring was lovely, but somehow it resolved everything she felt about Tyler. "Thank you, Tyler. You've been very good to the children, but I cannot marry you. I must also return your emerald. It belongs in your family."

Kerry pulled it off and passed it over with almost no regrets.

"But why?"

"Oh, Tyler, I don't know. I feel like a different person since I've come to India. These missionaries and students have such a wonderful working relationship with God. I had forgotten how marvelous that can be, and I'm trying to renew my walk with God. Your lifestyle doesn't seem to go along with that, does it?"

Tyler looked uncomfortable.

"I haven't been a church member in years," he acknowledged.

"Well, I haven't either, but what I was referring to is more personal than that. I'm interested in talking to God, trying to please Him and letting Him forgive me for my sins, so that I feel happier," Kerry explained simply.

Tyler stared at her, but Kerry couldn't read his expression. "I hope we can still be friends," she ended sincerely.

Tyler didn't seem to be brokenhearted. He heartily pumped her hand in a vigorous gesture of friendship, and

Kerry wondered if he was going to promise to write. Had she really considered marrying him? She must have been out of her mind.

Mr. and Mrs. Jagasia, comparing notes on the dinner that same evening, privately decided that it had been a most interesting group. "I wonder when she will realize?" was Mrs. Jagasia's remark.

Her husband replied, "And they think our arranged marriages are terrible?" Then he laughed and kissed the mother of his many, many children on the nose.

# FOURTEEN

**TYLER AND HIS LAWYER** greeted Kerry the next morning at the breakfast table.

"Kerry, my dear, we will finalize the trust with signatures of witnesses today. That way you can carry the agreement back with you and present it to the judge, who will decide guardianship of the girls in my favor, I hope."

Kerry felt better this morning after resolving the marriage issue with Tyler, but she hated to think that she would not see the children once they moved back to India.

The lawyer, a short, bland man, was stirring his eggs and bacon around on his plate like a bad-looking stew. He shook Kerry's hand limply and tried to make conversation. "I, uh, understand that you work for the same company that the Gundersons, uh, did work for, uh, yes?"

"Yes, I do. That's why I'm here."

"Oh. She was, uh, lovely, and so nice, that Mrs., uh, Gunderson," he finally got out.

"You knew her, too?" Kerry asked.

The lawyer stopped his fork in arc before putting it into his mouth, stringing yolk goo on the tablecloth. He paused, dripping, and said, "Well, of course. They did, uh, Tyler's survey right before they disappeared. We had lunch with them, the, uh, grown-ups, that is," he jerkily finished and pushed his food into his mouth.

Kerry couldn't watch him. She turned to Tyler. "Tyler, you never mentioned that the Geraghty and Miller work was done by the Gundersons." The Ohio office hadn't mentioned that either when she'd asked about the report that she'd seen on Tyler's desk.

"Kerry, I didn't want to upset the children. This is a fairly small white community here in New Delhi, and we were bound to meet each other. After all, it was only a professional relationship."

Somehow, Kerry felt very unsettled by this revelation. However, she did know that the soil report from Tyler's property had been routine. One of Mr. Miller's assistants had pulled up the results from the computer database and read them to her over the phone. The Gundersons' names, as technicians, wouldn't have been significant to him. No, there were no mysteries there.

Tyler dropped his teacup and saucer with a clatter as a low, moaning chant could be heard from the front of the house. The people from the local Hindu temple were coming!

Kerry ran to the kitchen and found Mrs. Peters calmly presiding over the children, who were well into making cut-out cookies. Mrs. Peters nodded gravely to Kerry, knowing her role as guardian dragon during the confrontation outside. "Have no fears, Miss Carlyle, the girls and I will have some wonderful treats for your dinner. After we bake these, we will be decorating them with icing and candies. It will probably take a long, long time. And then we will be raiding the attic for some more dress-up clothes."

Kerry smiled her thanks and ran out through the garden and across to the back door of the school. One young student directed her upstairs to the ladies' dorm, and she joined the other female students, looking out the windows onto the front courtyard and street below.

Kerry wiggled into the group to get a glimpse and inhaled sharply. Below, hundreds of men filled the street. Many carried tall tridents with marigolds twined around them. Others were smeared with ash, and all were chanting, swaying, and looking hostile. No one entered the courtyard, honoring an imaginary line between two different worlds.

In the courtyard stood Rand, looking relaxed now that the confrontation was finally here. He wore simple jeans and an open-necked white shirt, and stood tall, hands on hips, with all the male student body behind him. Lera, the small-statured evangelist, also had come to stand with them.

Kerry thought Rand looked very strong, and her heart felt as though it would burst.

A loud trumpeting sound made everyone turn to look down the street. Men parted to make a path for a great elephant, painted with white designs on her ears, forehead, and down the trunk. Heavy silver bracelets adorned the elephant's ankles, and on her back perched a large statue.

The painted plaster image was of a long-haired Oriental sitting cross-legged on a bull with a snake around his neck. For an idol, it looked garish and poorly executed to Kerry. Someone had draped it in shiny cloth and put flowers in its hair.

Minnie, next to her, filled her in on some facts. "This Hindu temple worships Shiva, the Destroyer. They call him that because they believe he destroys the world from time to time so it can be created again. He is known for his quick temper."

"In what way?" Kerry asked with some trepidation.

"Well, he supposedly beheaded his son, and when his wife got angry, he replaced his son's head with the head of the first living thing he came across, an elephant. You have seen images of the elephant-headed Ganesh?"

"Yes, they are quite eye-catching," Kerry agreed, wondering if servants of Shiva beheaded their rivals.

The elephant reached the entrance to the courtyard and stopped. From behind the big plaster statue jumped a wild-eyed man clad only in a *dhoti*, or loincloth, and covered in white ash from head to toe. His eyes were blackened with kohl, as were his lips and three long stripes from one side of his forehead to the other. Red dots showed up here and there on his skin, and some type of symbol was drawn in red on his chest. The three stripes in black appeared again and again on his upper arms, wrists, and elbows.

As soon as he appeared, arms raised, the crowd became silent. Their silence was more frightening than their loud chanting.

Kerry and the women watched, hardly daring to breathe, as the *sadhu*, or holy man, climbed down from the elephant and stood in front of the crowd at the entrance to the courtyard. There were hundreds of men with the *sadhu*, and hundreds more had quickly gathered from all over the neighborhood to watch. In comparison, only a handful of students stood in the courtyard behind Rand.

Yelling, the *sadhu* made a motion, and the crowd parted to bring out several twisted bodies of ascetics. They were placed on the ground, like sacks of laundry, unable to stand, their bodies and lives given to painful positions to obtain purity. The *sadhu* yelled at Rand, pointing and waving his arms and dancing around the prostrate bodies.

Rand spoke to him calmly in Hindi, and Minnie whispered the interpretation to Kerry up at the window.

"The *sadhu* says to look at the power those poor men have with their gods, to sacrifice so much. Rand says that he and his friends, the missionaries, have come to help the cripples become strong, not turn the healthy into cripples."

The *sadhu* spit into the courtyard but did not cross the invisible line that separated them.

Then the ascetics were literally shoved aside, as ten *fakirs*, or religious magicians, sat down in a line in front of the courtyard's entrance. They had many baskets, and all began playing on metal pipes, swaying and moving their bodies. With their feet they pushed off the lids of their baskets, and Kerry saw many snakes appear, most of them cobras with their hoods spread.

She felt faint and thought of Moses in the Egyptian court so many centuries ago. She wished she had the rod of Moses to eat up all those snakes.

Many fakirs took their fists and nudged or irritated their snakes, but the snakes didn't bite them. One man in the middle was charming three snakes in the same basket. Without stopping, he made a quick motion with one hand

and a young boy appeared out of the crowd. The child put his face near the basket and even touched one of the snakes with his cheek.

Kerry unconsciously clenched Minnie's arm. "Do you see that? He'll be killed!"

Minnie smiled and said, "It is a very old trick. The boy will be fine. I have seen it all my life, on the streets. They are trying to increase superstition by saying that it is magic, but the snakes do not feel threatened, and they are not hungry."

Sure enough, there was the boy, standing behind the *fakir*, who passed him a rupee.

The holy man pointed and screamed at Rand again, challenging him.

"He is daring Rand to come and pick up a snake. Now Lera answers. He says that his God made those snakes, and they crawl on their bellies because they have tempted God's children before," Minnie whispered.

This apparently made the holy man very angry, because he turned to the crowd, yelling directions. The crowd began raising their tridents and chanting, but this time they shouted and made a great noise.

The holy man turned and laughed at Rand, Lera, and the students. Then he reached into a pouch on his waist and pulled out a handful of something. He threw it into the courtyard, and dust exploded in front of Rand. Rand grabbed his eyes and fell to his knees. The other students looked bewildered. There was no fire.

They had not heard any explosion, and there was no evidence that there had been one. Yet they all saw the puff of dust and the doctor rubbing his face.

Rand, his eyes watering, staggered back to his feet and

said something to the holy man, so quietly that Minnie had to strain to catch it. "He is telling the Hindu that even if he were to leave the country immediately, the people will remember that he treated them with kindness and love. He says that fear and force cannot hope to compete."

The *sadhu* was silent; the crowd had grown quiet.

A horrible, wailing scream came from the back of the crowd. A man ran forward, spitting and cursing and throwing mud at Rand and the students.

Others picked up mud from the streets and some rocks, but the *sadhu* held up his arm, and they all abruptly stopped. He pointed his arm at the man who had run forward and who was still in a frenzy. Suddenly the man collapsed, and Kerry could not tell if he was dead or unconscious.

The *sadhu* threw back his head calling something to his followers.

Minnie didn't interpret.

Kerry jostled her arm. "What is he saying?"

"He says that those who do not follow him, Shiva will destroy."

Lera spoke again, his voice raised to the crowd.

"He is telling them that in the Bible, men like that were healed and went back to their families to be real fathers," Minnie sighed.

The great elephant's *mahout* started to poke and prod the animal, moving it back. The crowd began moving away from the courtyard. Even the holy man was taking steps away, although he wore an evil grin.

"What are they doing? Are they leaving?"

Minnie shook her head. "I don't think so. I don't know what they're doing."

Suddenly, great explosions came from under the soil in the courtyard. It seemed as though mines were going off all at once. The women could see Lera and the students trying to get back in the school. Kerry saw Rand's body thrown to one side. Fires burned where each explosion had taken place, and she waited, each second an hour, to see if Rand moved. He painfully pushed himself up and ran in the house, trying to avoid more explosions.

Kerry and the women rushed downstairs and found the students unharmed. Only Rand had superficial flash burns on his arms. It was a miracle that there had been no more injuries than that. Rand's eyes still watered.

"I think he threw a small cap filled with a very hot chili powder. I'm sure I'll be all right," he was telling Gwen, who was checking him over.

Kerry stood back from them, not wanting to intrude.

The Hindus shouted in triumph outside and waved their tridents. The *mahout* turned the elephant around and started away from the scene when one last huge and horrible explosion sounded. One of the smaller, planted explosives went off under the jeep, and the gas tank went up. A child's thin scream came from near the burning vehicle.

They all ran to the courtyard entrance to find the boy who had helped the *fakir* with the snakes. His thin body lay in an odd position on the ground without any movement.

Rand got there first and leaned over the child's mouth but could hear no breathing. Gwen could not get a heartbeat as she touched her stethoscope to his chest. She gave a negative shake to her head.

The *sadhu* finally entered the courtyard, running to the child. When he saw the absolute stillness of the boy and the limbs lying at odd angles, he threw his head back and screamed.

Everything stopped. All his people watched, horrified, as the *sadhu* pulled the broken, lifeless body onto his lap, rocking and chanting.

Rand reached out and touched the boy's head and the *sadhu's* shoulder. With a quiet voice that seemed to carry all over the crowd, he said, "Let me try."

The *sadhu* stopped rocking and looked at no one but the child. Kerry wondered if it was his son.

Rand pulled the child off the lap and onto the hard earth, where buried explosives had been erupting minutes ago. Students could be seen putting out the fire in the jeep just a few feet away.

Rand tilted the boy's head back and cleared an airway, then lowered his mouth over the boy's mouth and nose, giving five quick, strong breaths. Moving down to the child's chest, he located the place where the ribs joined the bottom of the sternum and placed both hands, pushing the heart into pumping the oxygenated blood through the body.

Gwen asked formally, "May I help?" They immediately switched to two-person cardiopulmonary resuscitation.

Everyone watched, transfixed, as they worked for three or four minutes.

They stopped and Rand checked for a pulse, while Gwen checked for breathing. Both shook their heads no.

Lera, with no medical training in his background, stepped up to them and smiled sweetly. "Let me try," he echoed Rand's words.

Rand sat back with tears in his eyes. "It's too late, Lera. He's gone."

Lera nodded and then laid his hand on the boy's forehead, saying a very short prayer. When he was done, he smiled at Rand again. "Please? You will try again? I believe God will heal."

This time Gwen nodded, and she and Rand began the process all over. They cleared the airway, filled the lungs, and pumped the heart manually.

As Kerry watched, the boy's eyes fluttered and he coughed. Then he rolled over and vomited on the ground. Rand and Gwen were smiling like idiots. The students cheered.

The *sadhu* wept, big streaks appearing in the ashes on his face. Kerry watched Rand very intently. He looked exhausted but thrilled.

The men in the streets and even the elephant were quickly leaving, not ready to tangle with any more powers today. Soon, only the *sadhu* and the boy remained.

Gwen was checking the child's reflexes, pupils, and skin. She sent students for splints and a stretcher, for several of his bones were broken.

The Hindu man stood and bowed very low to Rand and Lera.

Kerry quickly moved over next to Minnie to get the words. "The boy was his only grandson. He is begging Rand to forgive him. He says, like Shiva with Ganesh, he must make amends. Rand is asking him to stop the vandalism. To this he agrees. He says they will no longer block the way for Rand and his students. He promises to leave the property alone and also stop harassing the neighbors who choose to attend church services or medical clinics."

Minnie continued, "Now Rand asks if he will also stop

the threatening letters and notes."

She stopped. Kerry nudged her and then had to nudge her again.

Looking at Kerry with eyes wide, she interpreted, "He says he did not send any letters."

# FIFTEEN

**KERRY PACKED** her bags, trying to ignore her burning, aching stomach and chest. Depression always felt like a lung transplant to her. The children's clothing and toys fit in another shoulder bag. They wanted to carry their favorite toys with them on the plane. Kerry had their new purses, filled with busy, busy activities hidden for presentation on the plane.

Kerry tried to prepare Danielle and Kathryn for this day of departure, but neither seemed to absorb the information.

Mrs. Peters was trying to show a stiff upper lip, which tended to deteriorate each time she found a stray item in the house and brought it up to the room to be packed.

Perhaps the thing that hurt the most was Rand's behavior. After that wild morning with the snakes, explosions, and miracle, he had avoided Kerry at all costs. In fact the only thing he said to her, when she tried to tell him how wonderful he'd been, was, "Miss Carlyle, your plane leaves tomorrow evening. If you're going, be ready at three o'clock. I'll hire a car."

And with that, he frowned at her and walked off,

staying absolutely out of sight for the rest of the day.

The children were spending their last morning with Tiptoe down at the water hole with their friends, washing him and having a big water fight. Kerry could see them from the Greysons' library window. The water was shallow now, because it was winter and there were no monsoons, but she still liked to make sure everyone was being careful and checked on them often.

Danielle was most vocal about not wanting to leave that day, because she felt her parents were in India. Only with greatest persuasion had Kerry been able to make her understand that she and Kathryn couldn't come back to India as Tyler's wards unless they went to the courts in the United States first.

What Kerry did not explain was that once Tyler was appointed guardian, only a judge could change the guardianship order, even if the Gundersons did show up. And that would depend upon their circumstances and whether they were under arrest.

Kerry felt ghastly. Her brain kept poking her, nagging her to remember or understand something that she had missed! But the harder Kerry concentrated on this, the more confused she became.

She had had her morning devotions, with prayer, but no solutions were revealed by heavenly bands of angels.

Tyler said good-bye that morning, because he would be out of town the rest of the day. He'd kissed the girls on their heads and promised that he'd have a big party and rent a camel for rides the minute they came back.

Danielle and Kathryn were only moderately interested in this. They had a difficult time imagining anything better than Tiptoe.

To Kerry, he wished the best of luck and pressed a hundred-dollar bill into her hand, saying it was for anything the children wanted, to make their time fly faster while they were gone. Kerry smiled at the gesture and wondered if Tyler did anything without promising a treat. It was a wonder that Gwen was well-adjusted and had given herself to serving others in the medical field. Or maybe there was a connection.

Mrs. Peters called out the back door, and two wet, muddy bodies showed up, dripping on the tiles of the kitchen. After shooing them back outside, Mrs. Peters turned the garden hose on them before she let them run upstairs to a steaming bathtub. Kerry supervised the shampooing, while Mrs. Peters got lunch ready.

"Do we really have to go today?" Danielle complained bitterly. "My parents might show up today."

"Then Mrs. Peters will give them my phone number and they will get in touch."

This is it, Kerry thought, when they were all dressed in the now hated and despised parachute dresses. Or at least, Kerry had begun to despise them. The little girls still thought they were pretty cool, but they didn't own three of them.

Mrs. Peters made a memorable late lunch. Because Tyler wasn't there, she made Indian food and showed that she had quite a flair for it. Kerry wondered what Mrs. Peters did with her free time. She hadn't acquired this cooking from a book.

Gwen said good-bye that morning, leaving the same time as her father, because she had a village clinic way out in the rural north.

She was really very nice, Kerry had to concede, which

only made things worse. No wonder Rand was attracted to her. Not that Kerry had any interest in what Rand did.

She told herself that she would be glad to leave this place behind. She hadn't liked Rand or his bossy ways from the first, and he certainly hadn't liked her. There was no profit in thinking about that night in the kitchen, when she felt as though her heart would burst. It had probably been indigestion.

Kerry knew that Rand was dedicated to helping the fascinating people of India, and who better to assist than another dedicated person, Dr. Gwen?

Kerry felt even worse.

They waited while three o'clock came and went. Finally, Kerry and the children walked over to the school to see why the hired car was delayed. They found Rand pulling on his short hair and talking excitedly on the phone.

Minnie explained, "The hired car has not shown up. We are not able to find transportation to the airport."

Rand held his hand over the receiver and whispered to Kerry, "Is Tyler's car available?"

Kerry shook her head and said, "No, he's out of town."

"Gwen and her jeep?"

Kerry shook her head again and said, "Clinic up north."

Rand groaned and went back to the phone conversation.

"Why don't we call a taxi to pick us up?" Kerry asked Minnie.

"This is not the way in India. Most cabs have no radio, so you must flag them down in the business districts, which are an hour's walk from here."

Danielle was tugging on Rand's sleeve.

"Danielle, don't interrupt," Kerry chided.

"Rand, use Tiptoe. She'll give us a ride."

Rand stopped abruptly and looked at her. "You're right! Good thinking, Danielle. Tiptoe can get us to the business district in half the time, so that we can catch a taxi."

He and the children ran out of the office and left Kerry there, looking after them and saying, "You've got to be kidding. An elephant?"

She walked back over to the Greysons', where Mrs. Peters stood in the front courtyard with their bags. When she explained the crazy idea, Mrs. Peters laughed and clapped her hands. "Splendid!" she said. "I always love an elephant ride. It's a good experience for you, my dear."

Kerry thought Mrs. Peters didn't quite fit the mold of conservative grandmother after all. She was too adventurous.

Suddenly, around the corner of the courtyard came Tiptoe, who was at least six feet tall at the shoulder. Perched on top were the *mahout*, right behind the head, and then Danielle, Kathryn, and Rand sitting in the antique *hoodah*.

Tiptoe obligingly put her trunk down, and the *mahout* slid down and showed Kerry how to put her foot in the middle of the trunk for a step up. Rand slid off the back and came around to assist.

As soon as Kerry put her foot on the trunk, the elephant boosted her up. Kerry sort of scrambled over the head, between the eyes and ears, and crawled over like a monkey until she was situated on the hard edge of the curtained pagoda house. The whole contraption sat like a saddle on Tiptoe and was held in place with wide webbing around the neck and under the front legs of the elephant.

Rand passed the two shoulder bags to Kerry. The young *mahout* gave him a leg up onto the back of Tiptoe. Rand sat behind Kerry and hung one piece of luggage over his shoulder while she held the smaller bag, on loan from Mrs. Peters. Rand matter-of-factly reached forward and put his arm around her waist.

Danielle already had both of her arms around her little sister, and Kerry realized that they would all have to hold onto each other as they started to turn and walk away. Tiptoe was like a giant rocking chair that moved from side to side. The *hoodah* swayed and tipped precariously, only to right itself on the next step of the elephant. The ride was bumpy on the high, ridged back of an Asian elephant, so different from the wild African elephant's slightly swayed back.

They waved until Mrs. Peters was out of sight. She blew kisses and wiped her eyes every few minutes.

The reality of good-bye was settling in. Up until now, the girls had enjoyed the prospect of riding Tiptoe into town. Now, with Mrs. Peters out of sight, they became unusually quiet.

Kerry was horrified to feel tears rising in her eyes. She couldn't give in to self-pity now. Not when she was so close to Rand, his arm firmly holding her in the *hoodah*, which threatened to spill them any minute.

Gallons of water seemed to be gathering to spill over the rims of Kerry's eyes. She held herself very still and tried to open her eyes wider to accommodate the liquid.

Drain, you miserable tear ducts, she commanded. Don't betray me. I'd like to avoid looking more ridiculous than I already have.

Rand felt a big drop of water splash on his arm. He looked up, but there were no clouds. Another one hit his hand, and he leaned to the side to see Kerry, looking as bored and unconcerned as a Buddha, with rivulets of tears flowing from each eye.

Her brave face, when she was obviously upset, touched him more than anything.

He patted her shoulder and said some very comforting words: "Don't worry, you'll be back with Tyler before you know it."

It was the "old buddy" pat and the cajoling voice that gave Kerry the ability to pour her sorrow into anger. "Don't pat me again like some old spaniel!" she growled, sitting up straighter, if that was possible. "I'm not coming back. I'm not marrying Tyler, and I won't ever, ever see any of you again! So don't patronize me! And hold onto the tail, because I don't want your arm around me."

Rand sat back. She wasn't marrying Tyler? Come to think of it, she wasn't wearing that horrible ring today.

On the other hand, she sounded pretty glad to see the last of him, too. But she hadn't minded his arm around her a few minutes ago. In fact, she'd felt just right and relaxed.

Kerry's mood affected the children. They began to cry. Danielle, sure-footed as a mountain goat, stood and climbed over Kerry to sit in Rand's lap, while Kerry pulled the sniffling Kathryn into her lap for some mutual comfort.

Danielle sobbed, "If we leave, I won't ever find my mom and dad."

All this sorrow affected Tiptoe profoundly, who put her trunk over her head and ran the pointed tip down the length of Danielle and Kathryn's legs as they cried. Like a careful hand, it kept touching them.

Rand started to talk about elephants to distract the three weeping females. "Look, ladies! Tiptoe is doing the perfect thing to soothe baby elephants and also human children. A mother elephant runs her trunk over her baby's head, back, and legs to calm him down and let him know that she loves him. She also uses her trunk to greet other family members. They twist and twine their trunks together like a big hug. Elephants are very affectionate. Why, you've become her family! Your nose isn't getting any longer, is it?"

His silly banter helped, and he soon had the girls checking their noses and trying to pet Tiptoe's trunk.

They'd entered the marketplace with all the stands and shops when Tiptoe stopped and fanned her ears, moving her head from side to side.

Rand spoke to the young *mahout*, who answered in Hindi.

"What is it?"

"He says that the elephant is listening, but he does not know what she hears. Elephants hear things that none of us can hear. It is common knowledge among those who train elephants that they can hear another elephant who is thirty or forty miles away, through the lower vibrations of sound."

Tiptoe was perfectly still for several minutes; then she took off at a run in the wrong direction.

A big elephant walking slowly in India brings many smiles and gazes, but a running elephant causes people to panic. Crowds run and scream, shouting, "Musth, musth!"

Rand knew they thought the elephant was crazed, but

he had seen none of the other signs that would lead up to that season in this animal.

The *mahout* was poking Tiptoe in a sensitive spot behind the ear with his pointed stick to get her to stop, but she still ran. The amazing part was that Tiptoe did no damage. She side-stepped around children and wagons and even dogs. She didn't seem out of control, just fast.

Finally, in a small street, she ran toward the end of an alley and up to a vegetable stand. Tiptoe reached into the stand with her trunk, behind the tables of tomatoes and limes. Bringing her trunk up, she effectively pulled the material off the top of the building, for it was a temporary structure of canvas and poles, like a square tent.

People ran in all directions out of the small space. Like rats, they scurried down alleys and into doorways, disappearing from sight.

Tiptoe flung the canvas to the side, with the deft strength of her trunk and then put her head back and trumpeted.

Two people were left in the shambles of the pole and canvas structure. Their pale faces stared in shock at the elephant, but they did not run. They could not, because their hands and feet were bound.

The Gundersons!

# SIXTEEN

**THE CHILDREN SQUEALED;** Rand and Tiptoe trumpeted.

Before anyone could get off the elephant, an Indian in Western clothing ran up to the tent. He was wearing a draped turban, which looked incongruous to Kerry with his Western white shirt and tie.

He darted over to the bound couple, spoke only a word or two to Mr. Gunderson, and ran off.

Rand slid down the elephant's tail while the *mahout* climbed down the trunk. They cut the Gundersons' taped wrists and ankles as Kerry gently lowered the girls over the side. They could hardly wait, so she gripped their hands and leaned over the side of the *hoodah*, her leg wound around the wooden seat as they dangled and dropped the last foot. Danielle went first and grabbed her little sister's waist to cushion the landing. Then they raced toward their mom and dad.

Finally, Kerry climbed down the trunk by herself, thankful for Tiptoe's patience and cooperation.

The Gundersons ran to grab their daughters, and everyone spoke, hugged, and cried at once.

Tiptoe's *mahout* was apologizing, telling his marvelous elephant how beautiful she was. She was the best and smartest friend in all of India. Tiptoe accepted this apology with great aplomb as he fed her spilled tomatoes, kumquats, and mangos from one of the tables. There was no sign of the criminals who had kept the Gundersons in their shop.

Mrs. Gunderson, acting much like a mother elephant, was running her hands all over her children to make sure they were all right and to reassure herself that they were really here.

Mr. Gunderson was talking earnestly to Rand, relaying that the Indian man who ran up to him and spoke was from the police.

"He said, 'Police! We'll meet back at the Bible school,' and nothing else. What Bible school?"

Rand introduced himself and tried to give Mr. Gunderson a quick background of all that had happened in the last two weeks.

There was not room for all of them on the elephant, so Rand and Mr. Gunderson walked alongside while the ladies rode back to the Bible school in Tiptoe's *hoodah*.

When Rand and Kerry could see the school, they realized that it was a hive of activity, with police and official cars in the courtyard. They were surprised to see the state inspector, Mr. Rupa Das there, with many uniformed men spilling over into the courtyard of the Greysons next door.

Tyler stood by one of the police cars, back from his out-of-town trip, while two officers questioned him. Several other officers hurried over to the Gundersons, taking down names. Rand and Kerry stood with them in a huddle.

Finally the Indian they had all seen at the market-place, in his draped turban but wearing Western clothing, came over.

Kerry thought he looked familiar but couldn't place him. He addressed her, smiling broadly and bowing from the waist. "Miss Carlyle," he said in perfectly accented Oxford English, "it is a great delight to renew my friendship with you. Do you remember me perhaps?"

Kerry hesitated, looking closely into his smiling eyes. Her own eyes widened and she gasped, "No!"

"Oh, yes!" he nodded. "I believe I owe you a dinner, since you provided one to me."

The state inspector came over and shook everyone's hands. "I see you have met our best undercover agent," he laughed.

Rand looked puzzled, but Kerry explained. "He was the Naga. I saw him again at the village where we had church services. I couldn't imagine how he got there so quickly."

"It is an effective disguise and requires no costume," he explained, looking mischievous. "When people see a militant, naked man, they leave him pointedly alone and do not look at him closely. Also, when I put on Western clothing or a *kurta* and *jodhpurs*, no one associates me with the tribal people. But you, Miss Carlyle, looked me straight in the eyes and had compassion for a hungry man. It fixed me in your mind. I've had to be very careful since then to stay out of your sight."

"You've been following me?"

"We have always felt that someone would contact you or the children. We were on the right track."

"But no one ever contacted us."

"No, not you."

His eyes shifted over to Tyler, who was being hand-cuffed.

"They were trying to make a deal with Mr. Greyson," Mr. Rupa Das explained.

"With Tyler?"

"Yes, he hired them in the first place. But I will explain more fully, after we've taken your statements. Would you mind doing that now? If I can use your office, Dr. Dennison?"

The Gundersons followed Mr. Rupa Das into the school.

Rand and Kerry walked over to the Greysons' court-yard very slowly. Mrs. Peters was outside, wringing her hands. Gwen had just pulled up, tired and dirty from the day, and was standing there looking bewildered by it all. Rand went over, put his arm around her, and began to tell her a little of what had happened.

Kerry felt compassion with twinges of jealousy, watch-ing Rand with his gestures of kindness and comfort for Gwen. She went over and stood with her friend, Mrs. Peters. The older woman couldn't believe that Mr. Greyson had been arrested.

Mr. Hansa Rupa Das came back from the school, leav-ing the Gunderson family together in the garden. He explained that he had not really been inspecting Rand but Tyler all along. Then he asked Rand, Kerry, Mrs. Peters, and Gwen to come into the living room of the Greysons' house. Tyler wanted to make a statement for the police and them before they took him to be charged.

Sitting apprehensively, they watched as Tyler was led in, still dressed impeccably and looking unharried in his morning coat, but with the addition of handcuffs.

He nodded to each of them very formally and began. "I would like to apologize and explain some of this to each of you, if you will permit me. I am aware that the police clerk is taking this down as a statement."

Gwen looked white around the lips but nodded to her father to continue.

"I hired some men to steal a soil report from the Gundersons' home," Tyler began, "but it turned into a nightmare."

Mr. Rupa Das positioned his tape recorder to pick up Tyler's confession.

"Several months ago I hired the Gundersons, through Geraghty and Miller's British office, to assess the soil on my property. The results were amazing, so I called them to come and do more soil samples from the properties adjoining mine."

"The Bible school?" Rand asked.

"Yes," Tyler nodded, "but it is illegal to take soil samples without the owner's permission, so I told the Gundersons that I rented the property to you. I think they were suspicious, but they took the samples anyway."

Tyler looked at his immaculate hands as he spoke. "I wanted to steal and read their report before they had a chance to research the deeds and titles and present the report to the real owner, Rand. The school's report was better than my own, so I thought I would frighten Rand into selling quickly by sending threatening notes."

Rand frowned. "I do not own the property. I gave it to the Bible school. However, I am on the board of trustees."

Tyler didn't comment, but went on with his own story. "Unfortunately, the thugs I hired felt that if I would pay for the report, I would also pay for the Gundersons, and they kidnapped them."

Gwen looked bewildered at all this, but to Kerry's mind it sounded consistent with the impulsive, manipulative Tyler she had come to know.

"I was horrified when they first called and told me that they had the Gundersons and I must pay a ransom. I was afraid to pay because I felt they were ruthless, and once they had the money they might have no more use for their victims and kill them. I stalled, trying to negotiate a ransom, and paid a private detective agency to trace them. It was the agency's idea to 'burglarize' the Gundersons', looking for some clues to their whereabouts left by the kidnappers. The contents of the house are in one of my warehouses by the factory."

So that was where Bubbles got the family photo and Mrs. Gunderson's passport, Kerry reasoned.

Tyler smiled tightly, still looking at his pristine fingernails. "I couldn't believe my luck when Rand asked if the Gundersons' children could stay with us. I would know that the children were safe, and maybe I could make some of this dreadful calamity up to them. Also, if the Gundersons were never recovered, an unfortunate fact in some kidnappings, I could provide a home, future education, and some love for them."

Kerry thought how naive Tyler was, for all his sophistication.

Gwen looked crushed. Rand held her hand, but she seemed unaware of his presence. "Oh, Dad," she sighed.

"Gwen," Tyler said in a whisper, "I am so sorry that I've embarrassed you and caused each of you sorrow. I tried to undo my evil to the Gundersons, but I could not.

My only consolation is that the Gundersons are found, and Danielle and Kathryn are happy again. They are wonderful children."

Gwen went to her father, standing next to him in loyalty. They all stood as he was escorted to the waiting police car. Gwen called their lawyer from the library and then followed in her jeep. Rand offered to go with her, but she asked that he honor her desire to be alone for this task.

When she was gone, Mrs. Peters asked Kerry to please continue and use the guest room for the night. She asked if Rand and Kerry would please excuse her, for the shock of Tyler's arrest had made her very tired and she was going to lie down for a while.

Rand excused himself, going back to the school, so Kerry was alone.

She carried her bags to the guest room and immediately knelt to pray. First, she offered thanksgiving. Her heart was so grateful for the reunited Gundersons! Then she prayed for forgiveness, for her anger was great against Tyler's greed. Then, when she felt the anger ebb away, she found herself praying for Gwen and Mrs. Peters. She felt empathy swell in her heart, for they were suffering greatly.

Kerry knelt there a long time, looking for comfort and direction. When she finally stood, much later, Kerry looked different. She no longer looked confused. She had something to offer when she knocked on Mrs. Peters's door, interrupting the older woman's weeping.

Gwen dragged herself in, late that evening, to find that Kerry and Mrs. Peters were waiting for her with a hot meal, strength, and hope.

Rand also sought the refuge of prayer in his office at

the school. He prayed throughout the night, seeking God's will. But God did not reveal the future or a specific plan of action to Rand. He put his life in God's hands blindly as he had many times before, knowing that he could trust the Creator. But Rand was still human enough to wish that just once God would let him know what he could expect.

It was a tired but calm Rand who knocked at the Greysons' the next morning to pick up Kerry for her departure. The Gundersons insisted on going along to the airport, because they were so grateful for Kerry's part in watching over their children.

The adults sat on benches at Kerry's gate in the airport, discussing Tyler's confession. Mr. Gunderson, tall, with typical Scandinavian blond looks, was explaining the soil reports. "When we found indications of beryllium aluminum silicate, we wondered if it might be colored by chromium, which we also found in trace deposits."

Rand and Kerry looked blankly at him, so he explained. "Emeralds. We think there might be emeralds on the property."

Kerry gasped.

"Well?" Rand asked eagerly.

"Well, I don't know. It's fully possible to have a vein of beryl and traces of chromium on the same property. The real question is, did the chromium ever combine with parts of the beryl to color it with enough green to make any of the plain beryl into an emerald vein? Even if you have emeralds, there are wide ranges of color and value on the market."

"Rand," Kerry asked, suddenly excited. "Do you know if Tyler's family have lived in that house a long time?"

"Of course. His great-grandfather built the house during the heyday of the East India Trading Company."

"The ring! I wonder if that emerald came from their property? It was his grandmother's. It also might explain his extravagant spending."

Rand sadly shook his head. "I'm afraid not. Tyler is overwhelmed in debt, Gwen's just found out. That's one of the reasons he was so anxious to buy the school property and have sole rights to emeralds in that area."

"But he bought all sorts of things, like cars and elephants. What will happen to Tiptoe?" Kerry wanted to know, worried about the fate of the animal.

"And how did she know where to find us?" was Mr. Gunderson's question.

Kerry explained how Tiptoe had stopped and listened at the market, after soothing the crying children.

"You don't think she could hear me crying, do you?" Mrs. Gunderson asked.

"I know that there is something very special about a mother elephant who has lost her own baby and adopts two little blond girls who have lost their mother. We may never really know how she did it," Rand concluded.

Mrs. Gunderson nodded slowly. "I've read articles about biologists who have researched elephant language. They claim that elephants can hear each other from many miles away and that they are especially sensitive to distress calls. But I always thought it was a bit farfetched, until now." Kerry said she thought it was an amazing miracle, and the second one she'd seen that week!

Mr. Gunderson thought he knew Tyler's original motive behind the purchase of the elephant. "I think Tyler planned on the elephant excavating the property and helping to mine the emeralds. They're certainly considered work animals and require no permit, unlike big earth-moving equipment. If you had the patience and wanted to keep your emerald source a secret, Tiptoe, aptly named, might be the perfect solution."

Mrs. Gunderson was watching her children play nearby, next to the window. They had beads or marbles on the floor and were playing some sort of game. She wandered over to see, unable to resist touching and patting them over and over.

"What do you have, petite chou?" she asked Kathryn, using a family endearment, which meant "little cabbage."

Kathryn passed her the pebbles she had collected as treasure.

Mrs. Gunderson swallowed and held them up in the sunlight, gasping and laughing.

Kerry, Rand, and Mr. Gunderson looked up when she ran over.

"Look!" She held the children's pebbles loosely in her hands. Then she held them up to the light streaming in from the windows. Her hands glowed a deep dark green, as though lit from within by a green fire.

There was a moment of silence, and then they all began to speak at once, excitedly.

Suddenly Mrs. Gunderson asked her husband in an alarmed voice, "Was any iron found in your report?"

Kerry caught the apprehensive note in her voice. "Why? What difference would it make? These are emeralds, right?"

"Not if they're colored green by iron," she explained. "Then they're just worthless green beryl, not emeralds."

Mr. Gunderson was grinning. "Not a trace anywhere.

210

Those are emeralds. Let's find out where the children found them."

Rand asked, "Do you think I could use Tiptoe to get emeralds? They would certainly help pay for books, supplies, a few clinics, and the purchase of a marvelous elephant."

Upon questioning, Danielle and Kathryn remembered digging their pebbles out from the banks of the mud hole while they washed Tiptoe.

"That's her most favoritest place to roll in the mud, and we like it, too," Kathryn said, in a full sentence, with perfect enunciation if not perfect grammar.

Kerry and Rand stared at her. Her parents didn't seem surprised.

Danielle explained. "Mom, she hardly talked at all while you were gone. It was a big vacation for me," and she rolled her eyes like all long-suffering sisters do.

They all broke into laughter, until Kathryn got self-conscious and hid behind a chair.

Rand made arrangements to get together with Mr. Gunderson at the school the next day. Mrs. Gunderson thanked Kerry and Rand again and again for their watchful care, especially after Danielle told her about their own attempted kidnapping.

Mr. Gunderson was wearing his watch and ring again, having collected them from the police. He'd inconspicuously dropped them in the garden as they'd been hurried away, hoping someone would find them and realize that they'd been abducted.

The children hugged Kerry and seemed sad to say good-bye, but they were obviously relieved to have their parents back. The Gundersons discreetly slipped off to get a snack downstairs, after thanking Kerry again and saying good-bye.

Kerry wiped her eyes, which were a little moist, knowing that the chances were almost nonexistent that she would ever get to see the children again.

Rand cleared his throat. "You know, Kerry, I have been much impressed by the strength of character and presence of mind that you have shown during this whole adventure."

Well, I never would have guessed it, Kerry thought.

"In the face of many frightening and unexpected turns, you were of great comfort to the children and of some help to me." I sound like I'm getting ready to present the Purple Heart or something, Rand thought, unsure of how to get to a less formal verbal avenue. "I think that you would be a valuable helper to the ministry here in India, and I would like for you to consider such." There, I've gotten it out, he inwardly sighed.

Kerry's head jerked up. "What about Gwen?"

"Gwen doesn't want to teach at the school. Besides, she's getting ready to go up north, possibly into Nepal."

"Aren't you going?"

"Me? No, I'm not part of that medical expedition. Why would I go?"

Right, Kerry thought, why would he go? He's not romantically interested in Gwen, I knew it all along. They're just friends. Besides, he's just proposed to me!

"Rand, do you really want me?"

"The school body voted on it unanimously!"

"The school voted?"

"Oh, yes. Because they all knew you, I thought I would find out their feelings."

"Well, what if they had voted against me?"

"I hardly think you would have fit in as an administrative assistant if the students hadn't liked you."

Kerry quickly tried to remember all her words in the last few minutes. She hadn't slipped and said anything that would let him know her horrible mistake, had she? To think that she actually mistook a business arrangement for a proposal. Kerry's embarrassment overwhelmed her. She hoped she wouldn't cry.

Rand could see that he'd said exactly the right thing as Kerry smiled strangely at him. She must be so happy that she's afraid of showing me how grateful she is. What a dear! Rand waited for her acceptance.

"Oh, my," she said tightly. "Your thoughtfulness . . . and generosity are overwhelming. I'm almost speechless, but not quite. I am able to say, without hesitation, no."

With that Kerry reached out and gave his hand a brisk shake. Then she picked up her bag and turned her back on Dr. Dennison, creep of the week.

She gratefully saw people boarding her flight and walked through the doorway with a quick step.

Rand couldn't believe this. Where was she going? He was so sure that she was going to accept. She seemed to like him . . . at times. She wasn't going to marry Tyler! Where had he gone wrong? He couldn't let her leave!

Rand grabbed one of the flight attendants. "I need to speak to a woman who just boarded that plane. May I go on board?"

"Oh, no, sir. You can never go onto the plane without a boarding pass. Is it an emergency?"

"Yes. Yes, I think it is."

The stewardess went racing down the aisle of the plane, finding Kerry and rushing her out. They both ran back to the gate, Kerry thinking that some new disaster had struck.

"What is it, what is it?" she asked Rand breathlessly.

"I don't want to say good-bye, Kerry."

Kerry and the stewardess looked at him with steady stares.

In tones used for the violent and unstable, Kerry said, "All right, Rand. Let's just say au revoir or toodle-loo or ta ta, but we'll certainly avoid saying good-bye. O.K.?"

"Kerry, you don't understand." Rand moved closer. "Kerry, will you come back to India?"

"Well, Rand, I don't know."

"Kerry, I wish you could be here for the Festival of the Lights," he explained inadequately, sweating.

"Rand, I have to go."

"Kerry, do you like India?"

Kerry sighed. "Yes, Rand, I like India. Was there anything else?"

Rand felt paralyzed.

Kerry looked disappointed and slightly angry. She turned and walked back through the doorway and onto the plane.

Rand watched her go. What on earth was he doing? He'd almost proposed and then found he couldn't.

Rand watched the plane leave the tarmac, disappearing in the sky, and wondered how he would get her to come back.

Kerry felt too upset to cry. She sat staring out the window, seeing nothing. She thought of her routine back in Ohio and Gwen's unexpected offer last night. Suddenly, it seemed a great deal more attractive. She *would* accept the invitation to go to Nepal with Gwen's medical team!

Wouldn't Rand be surprised to know that she had other fish to fry!

The airline attendant instructed the passengers to look out the right side of the cabin to see the mountains.

Smiling an odd smile, Kerry looked at them a long time and wondered if her father knew any missionaries in Nepal.